HUNTING
TRUFFLES

Dick Rosano

ISBN: 1503088073
ISBN 13: 9781503088078
Library of Congress Control Number: 2014919798
CreateSpace Independent Publishing Platform
North Charleston, South Carolina

1

THE TRUFFLE MARKET
IN ALBA, ITALY

The heady aroma of white truffles filled the air in the cavernous marketplace. The sales floor was enclosed in a large makeshift tent which seemed to trap and accentuat the fragrance, but more likely it was simply the soulful scent of *tartufo bianco,* the little tuber memorialized in poems and culinary prayers around the world, that scented the air. The mouth-watering smell of this delectable condiment could send chefs into paroxysms of rapture, and cause diners to outspend their budgets.

"One thousand euros for half a kilo?" The man with the stubby beard behind the counter cast a cold glance at his customer. The merchant was tending a small collection of chalky knobs, clumps unearthed just hours earlier, fungi whose unremarkable appearance disguised the truffles' starring role in modern cuisine.

"*E' ridicolo!*" he exclaimed. "I wouldn't sell a half kilo of my truffles for less than two thousand euros!"

His neighbor, also tending a counter with dusty *tartufi* displayed like prized jewels in a glass case, chimed in.

"Si," he said with a belly laugh. He considered the visitor, someone obviously not from Italy, and certainly not from Piedmont, where everyone knows the value of fine truffles. "These little gems are worth more than you know, but I can shave some off of this little one for that thousand euros you seem anxious to spend."

The customer, properly chastised and spotted as an amateur among experts, blushed slightly, but he pointed to one of the smallest knobs in the second dealer's showcase.

"What does that weigh?" he asked uncomfortably.

The *trifolào*, or truffle hunter, hoisted the gnarly nugget between his thumb and forefinger, eyed it closely, then lowered it reverently onto a scale set along the side of the counter.

"About point-three kilo," he proclaimed, with his right hand facing down, fingers spread and waving back and forth. "Maybe nine hundred euros. You want?"

The startled customer was clearly taken aback. He had chosen the smallest truffle in the case and still couldn't imagine paying such a large sum for it. He had tasted the *tartufo bianco* before at restaurants and was admittedly smitten by it, and he wanted to take some back to the U.S. to treat his friends. But he couldn't bring himself to spend $1,000 for something so small.

"Why is it so expensive, when I can have it in restaurants without feeling like I'm spending too much money."

The two *trifolài* smiled at one another, but tried to explain to their new guest.

"Do you see those judges up there?" the second man asked, pointing to the raised dais where several men and women sat.

"Yes, I do," answered the visitor, hesitantly.

"They are judges. They make sure that everything sold in this market is truly, and clearly, the white truffle of Piedmont, the most prized culinary treasure in all the world, *tuber magnatum*. The restaurants, well, they may slip in some truffles from other regions, or even some of the Perigord truffles from across the border." He couldn't bring himself to say France, the source of black truffles, thought by most chefs as good, but not up to the quality of Italy's white truffle.

"And besides," added the first merchant, "the restaurant only shaves a tiny portion onto your plate, once, twice with a shaver, so there's not so much to have."

His counterpart was quick to add that truffles are so pungent that only a little is used in any case.

"In fact, even this tiny nugget of truffle here," he declared as he raised the one from the scale, "is actually enough to serve four or five people, for several meals. On pasta, risotto, omelette…*capisce?*"

The visitor was impressed, but he couldn't part with 900 euros, no matter how much he liked his friends. He bade the merchants goodbye and meandered away, breathing deeply of the breath-taking aromas before sheepishly exiting the market altogether.

2

A PRECIOUS GEM

Nestled in the hills of the Piedmont, Alba is an ancient city with centuries of tradition. It is not a fortified city, like many of those towns in Tuscany where the Florentines and the Sienese were constantly at war. No, Alba has the charm of a cozy village-city without the international flair of those Renaissance capitals.

The people of Alba know their place, they know that tourists with their millions of dollars wouldn't make a detour to their pleasant little hamlet, but the Albese know something else and take great pride in it.

The greatest and most expensive Italian wines come from the hills that surround Alba. There is Barolo – called the King of Wines, and Barbaresco – the Prince of Wines. But these merely set the standard for the brilliance of

Piedmontese viticulture. There are so many red wines made from the same nebbiolo grape, including Gattinara, Spanna, and Sizzano. Add to the list the great white wines of the Piedmont, like Arneis, Cortese, and a scattering of Pinot Grigio, and this tiny village of Alba could easily be crowned the seat of Italian wine royalty.

Of course, fabulous wine is always accompanied by equally fabulous food, and the Albese have also developed their own niche for food. Combining the seafood and olives from Liguria just to the south, the chefs in Piedmont added unique forms of pasta, beef, fresh produce, seafood from neighboring Liguria, and precious herbs to highlight the natural flavors of it all. From elegant restaurant dining rooms to pleasant home kitchens, the food of this region always delivered memorable meals.

And the Albese had one other thing that they were immensely proud of: truffles and the annual Truffle Festival that opened in late-September and carried on through the winter months until the harvest of the famed *tuber magnatum* had run its course.

Each year, crowds filled the streets of Alba in the days and weeks leading up to the festival. They were mostly European tourists - - for some reason the Americans hadn't truly embraced this culinary treasure yet. With its focus on truffles and the endless dishes that could be improved by including this ingredient, the festival was first and foremost a culinary event. But at the opening ceremonies, the Albese put on a Medieval show with costumed actors performing scenes from the Middle Ages, including grand parades, starving peasants, mock battles, even fake hangings. And there was the Palio degli Asini, or famed donkey race, fought with ferocity but a heavy dose of humor to determine which *borgo*, or neighborhood would reign for the year as the champions of the Festa del Tartufo. After the race, the Medieval actors and winners of the Palio marched through the city streets like a scene out of the 17th century, singing the praises of their heroic donkey and his intrepid rider.

The Albese knew they occupied a favored seat in Italy's wine, food, and cultural history. And they relished it.

3

WORKING THE VINEYARD
IN SINALUNGA

Three hundred miles away, in a dusty field in Tuscany, Paolo straightened up and arched his back, then leaned on the rake he had been scraping across the hardened earth at his feet. He took off his weather-beaten Washington Nationals baseball cap, stained from sweat and dusty from work, and fanned the muggy air to stir even a bit of breeze on his face.

It was mid-September, usually a time of some relief in the vineyard since the harvest was mostly completed, and Paolo was helping his father, Dito, clean the rows of vines to prepare them for their winter sleep. The pickers had moved on to other vineyard rows, and Dito had already arranged contracts to sell their grapes to surrounding wineries; that left father and son alone in the stillness of the vineyard to put everything in order for the period of hibernation that came with the chill winds of autumn.

Vineyards were places of magic in brightly colored wine brochures and travel posters, but the dell'Uco family knew them as places of work. Agriculture of any stripe could be hard, back-breaking work, an occupation that shared its destiny with the vagaries of the weather, and Paolo had grown into this family enterprise but still resisted letting it grow in his heart.

Dito had more years on him and more seasons in the vineyard. He had worked the fields for most of his adult life and, although the effort sometimes showed on his face, he never regretted it. His fruit would be bottled by other families who owned the wineries and Dito knew that these grapes would make fine wine.

Paolo yanked the hat back in place to shield his face from the sun and coughed a bit of dust from his throat. He was young and strong and he didn't intend to turn gray-haired and worn in this vineyard. The dell'Ucos would go on, but he had bigger thoughts, bigger dreams than filling the fermentation vats of the families who put their name on the bottles of wine.

Dito kept his head bent toward the ground and just kept raking the discarded grapes and random twigs and broken branches in the furrow between the rows of vines.

Paolo looked at his father with a slight dose of pity, and he was immediately embarrassed by the emotion. Still, he wondered why his father would want to spend his years growing someone else's wine.

He studied his father's stocky figure, a body that seemed well designed for farm work. His legs and arms were short but muscled, his strong neck was darkened by years of working outside, and the lines on his face were like the rivulets of time, chronicling the mixture of good times and bad, but most of all they served as a badge of honor for a man who had never let up in the relentless labor of farming.

Paolo wished his father would make the wine that his fruit would yield in someone else's *fattoria*, an inelegant Italian word for "farm" that was commonly used to refer to wineries across this storied land.

"I'm a farmer, not a winemaker," Dito always reminded him. Sometimes the declaration was made with chin held high, proud of his connection to the earth, but sometimes Dito's gaze dropped ever so slightly, the glitter of pride in his eyes a bit more subdued, enough that Paolo detected a note of sadness in his father's voice. Winemaking in Sinalunga, and the entire region of Tuscany around it, was a noble calling, an industry that is both science and art, and one that preserved a tradition of excellence that Italy promoted around the world. But in their little world between the vines here in Sinalunga, not far from Siena,

Paolo sensed that winemaking was out of their reach. The vineyard provided a steady income, but not the riches that would be required to build a winery and establish a wine-making enterprise.

"It doesn't matter, anyway," Paolo mumbled to himself. "I won't be here for long. I don't want to be here for long."

Dito was now the one to stand and stretch his sore back, stealing a glance in the direction of his son and only child. They exchanged a brief look, but Paolo shied away from the glance so that his father would not see him standing idle, as he bent back over the rake and returned to the dusty business at hand.

Paolo passed his time dreaming about his plans. He began his campaign with his mother almost a month earlier, suggesting in an off-hand way that he might want to go to America. There are things to do there, he said, "Maybe I'll discover what I want to be in life." Paolo was twenty-three years old, old enough to dream of a future different from the path his parents chose, yet young enough to let dreams override common sense.

At least that's how his mother, Catrina, put it the first time he raised the idea.

"America is a wonderful place," she said, never looking up from the laundry she was folding, "or so we're told. But we have no family there and your father needs you. What would you do in America until this great day when you 'discover what you want to be?'"

That put an end to the conversation, that day at least, but Catrina's words only convinced Paolo that he needed to think it through more thoroughly and come up with answers to the questions his mother would undoubtedly ask next time.

A few weeks later, Paolo was ready. He raised the subject again at dinner, daring to broach it in front of both parents. Dito didn't look up from his plate of pasta, and broke off mouthfuls of Catrina's freshly baked bread without raising his head to look at his son.

"I think I could go to America to visit, see New York and maybe Washington," Paolo began tentatively, touching the Nationals cap that he had hung on the chair beside him, as if it were some kind of talisman. His father still didn't acknowledge the conversation, but Catrina responded.

"That sounds nice. What would you do there?"

"Maybe, first, I could just visit. Maybe I would discover that there was something I could do there. And, maybe I would find a job," he replied, but his hesitation and string of 'maybes' proved that he still didn't have the answers.

The meal ended without Dito engaging the topic. When the food was eaten and the last glass of wine was poured, he stood and asked his son to bring the file on wine buyers in so he could look it over and plan next year's crop.

4

ROOTS IN THE VINEYARD

By morning, most of the vineyard work had been completed, and Dito called Paolo out to the field, ostensibly to check the wires supporting the vines, and one last cut through the rows to make sure everything was in order. Paolo knew that his father would be back nearly every day, and he surmised that Dito's real purpose was more personal.

So when Dito and Paolo started out that morning for the vineyard, they loaded a few tools into the truck and drove the few miles to their farm. There was something oddly reassuring about the creaky old truck that Dito refused to replace. The suspension was nearly gone, and it took more than a single turn of the key to fire up the engine, especially as the air cooled in autumn, and for all his misgivings Paolo smiled at the spirited debate his father had with *la macchina* while man and machine battled for dominance.

They pulled up to the fringe of the vineyard and *la macchina* came to a stop, almost as if it was annoyed by the braking action. Dito pushed the door open and turned sideways before lowering himself to the ground, a reluctant submission to a sore back weakened by years of farm labor. Paolo had more energy but silently stepped out of the truck, not wanting to aggravate his father's condition by showcasing the vigor of youth.

The old man stepped between two rows of vines as if these were his true family. Shy of a smile, his face nevertheless lit up as if he was more at home here than anywhere else in his existence.

Through most of the summer, Dito's hands were his closest connection to the soil. He watched, dug into it, pulled a handful toward his face to sniff it, and from this communion was able to discern the mystical fate of the vines under his care. He tended these vines and the earth, using his hands to get a sense of how things were going. It was this tactile connection to the earth that Dito seemed to love the most, as if his hands were translating the meaning of the soil for him.

But after the harvest when the grapes were gone and the leaves were turning yellow and brown on the vine, Dito relied more on his eyes, and that day he stood at the head of one vineyard row and surveyed the leaves rustling in the breeze. He stared off into the distance as the row climbed a rise, then disappeared over the hill. Paolo noticed the change in his father at this time of year, and it seemed that Dito was looking beyond the vines, beyond even his own life, peering into the future and the past at the same time, using his imagination to meld the two into the seamless totality that was life for Italians.

Then, he stooped and lifted a handful of dried earth, and smiled. Someone unfamiliar with vineyard work would have thought the dusty handful to be proof of a barren plot of land. But grapevines produced the best wine when their roots had to dig deep to find water. "Like our people," Dito sometimes said, "the best ones come from struggling to survive."

He didn't have to repeat those words to Paolo that day; he just looked at his son. And Paolo realized that his father's glance was his first response to the son's plea to go to America.

After only a short time in the vineyard, they climbed into the truck and drove back to their home in Sinalunga. Italians cherish the extended family and live among relatives throughout their lives. This concept of communal living even extends to the neighbors and villagers around whom many Italians shape their lives. So, unlike American farmers who build a home in the middle of a vast farm, miles from the nearest neighbor, Italians live in villages that are, themselves, surrounded by farmland. Many of those who own and tend the fields live in these villages and walk or ride their trucks out to the farmland and vineyards in the day, returning to their neighbors, friends, and family in the village at night.

Arriving home, Dito put the tools away and Paolo dutifully spent his afternoon cleaning the large garage that doubled as a farmer's shed. Each man was left to think about what each knew was uppermost in his mind.

That evening, the three sat at the table for dinner. From her small but functional kitchen, Catrina produced meals that would headline restaurants in other countries. But even in rural Italy, such exalted flavors were the hallmark of local cuisine. Fresh ingredients and local produce were the key, as well as simple cooking techniques that neither baked the flavors out nor blanketed them with sauces. Catrina had grown up in the kitchen and learned her many skills from the woman who bore nine children, all hungry, and all expecting to feast on the memorable foods of their homeland.

Evening repasts, called *cena* in Italy, were eaten earlier in the countryside than in the cities. Farmers began their work early in the day and tired early in the evening so, unlike their urban cousins, they would have their final meal of the day around seven o'clock then drift into a well-deserved sleep by nine.

After the vegetables were eaten, platters of meat would arrive. Tuscan kitchens were renowned for the luscious meats and fowl that emerged from them, broiled, boiled, roasted, grilled, and sometimes simply salted and dried. That night, Catrina brought out a steaming roast of pork, surrounded by links of cinghiale sausage, a regional favorite made from the meat of the local wild boar. The aromas of rosemary, sage, and garlic rose from the platter and Dito poured another glass of wine as if to toast the feast.

Dito, Catrina, and Paolo ate in an unusual silence, unusual because Italians consider mealtime to be the happiest and most convivial of social interludes. But tonight all three knew they were thinking about growing things, both grapes and children, and about America.

"Why do you want to..." Dito began, but before he could finish the sentence Catrina knew was coming, she interrupted him.

"Paolo," she said softly, and Dito immediately deferred to her. "When was the last time you saw Zia Rita?"

"Rita? Your sister?"

"Of course," Catrina said, loading more meat onto Dito's plate to keep him out of the conversation for another minute. "How many aunt Ritas do you have?"

"It's been a couple of years, I guess," Paolo replied. "Why?"

"Well, the grapes are in, and you're developing a bit of wanderlust, and I just thought that a trip to Genoa to visit your aunt might be just the right thing."

It wasn't that Paolo was that close to his aunt Rita, but he hadn't been the Genoa, "the City of Ships," since he was a young boy. He had learned more about it in recent years, and the city's reputation for ship-building and exploration, so maybe a few days – or more? – on Italy's Mediterranean coast might be exciting.

Dito continued chewing his dinner, but looked silently at his son, waiting for an answer, or at least some sign that Paolo was considering the idea. Dito didn't necessarily agree with Catrina's suggestion, he didn't even know it was coming, but he immediately understood its purpose, as a way to delay Paolo's broader ambition to travel.

"You could work in her restaurant," Catrina said, to fill in the silence and keep them on topic. "What do you think?"

"Si," Paolo conceded finally, "that would be a good idea. Papa, it's true the grapes are in. Do you need me here? I would only be gone a week, maybe two."

Dito had already decided to agree, but hid that fact under a guise of nonchalance. Waiting just a few seconds for effect, and to establish that his approval was the only one that really mattered, Dito raised his eyebrows and shrugged his shoulders, without stopping the mastication of the morsel of cinghiale sausage and without speaking any words. But with that gesture, he gave his consent.

5

IL BAR SPIRITI

The clink of glasses and conversation filled the air with sound at the wine bar at Il Bar Spiriti in the central piazza of Sinalunga. The smell of fresh flowers mingled with the aromas of juniper and lavender leaves that stood tall in vases around the room, entwined with the unmistakable aroma of wine in all its forms. Paolo came here often to visit his friend, Dante, who worked the counter at Il Bar and served wine and small snacks to a clientele that was mostly local, with only a few tourists discovering this neat little hideaway in the outskirts of the town.

Everything about the wine bar was different from Paolo's environment at home. Instead of the quiet sounds of a rural farmhouse, Paolo could enjoy the vibrant nightlife at this popular watering hole. And tonight, he had exciting news to give his friend.

"I'm leaving for Genoa next week," he began, thinking that this was less than a trip to America, but still better than working in the dusty expanse of a vineyard. "My aunt, Zia Rita, owns Ristorante Girasole and I thought I'd spend some time there, working in the restaurant and maybe spending my days on the beach."

"Sounds good," Dante said while drying and polishing some wine glasses behind the bar. He was tall and handsome, with a full head of wavy black hair, an athletic build, blue eyes, and a sculpted chin – a ladies' man – and he did little to cover for his enjoyment of this fact. Where Paolo was sensible and straightforward, Dante was flamboyant and imaginative. He saw the world as an opportunity to meet girls and have fun; Paolo imagined such a life but his rural upbringing kept him more grounded than his flashy friend.

"Maybe you'll need some help on the beach," said Dante, setting one glass down and raising another. "Maybe the girls there will be too much for you," he smiled and arched his eyebrows in the imagined pleasure.

"No, I'll be alright," Paolo said. He didn't want to let on that the trip was arranged by his mother and that it wasn't really a vacation.

"I'll be there a week or two, just now before the weather cools off. Should be a nice break from this place."

"What, you don't like Bar Spiriti?"

"Yes, I definitely like it here, and I like Sinalunga," Paolo said with a slight hint of regret. "I meant home." Paolo referred to his home with a flick of his head in the general direction of the dell'Uco farm that his family owned. "Genoa will be just what I need," he added, musing silently that a trip to Genoa was more important for his experiment in severing ties than it was for transient pleasure.

Paolo swirled the wine in his glass, took a thoughtful sip, then peered at the glass again.

"Si, it's Chianti," nodded Dante. "But can you guess from what estate?"

Paolo didn't like it when Dante played this game. He couldn't guess the provenance of the wine, his tastes were too simple for that. And he was sure that his friend couldn't either, but he played along.

"No. Where's it from?"

"An old estate named Castello di Gabbiano. They make a simple Chianti, a Chianti Classico, and a Chianti Classico Riserva. You have the Classico in your glass. Really something, huh?"

Paolo looked at him and said, "Yeah, but you wouldn't have known that if you weren't the one to pour the wine, right?"

Dante gave a sideways glance. He always tried to play the wine expert for the girls and the tourists, but there was no reason to try to fool his friend. He ended his brief glance with a playful smile, but otherwise didn't answer Paolo's question.

Instead, Dante's attention was drawn to two young women seated at the table right in front of his bar. They were trading stories in *sotto voce*, a muted voice, and looking his way. Dante didn't miss a chance to use his role as wine server in this establishment, and plied it often as an excuse to approach a table. He grabbed an open bottle of the Prosecco the ladies were drinking and swung into action.

"*Un po di piu?*" he asked.

"*No, grazie, this glass was enough*" said the one with auburn hair and green eyes. "Do you own this place?"

"Well, of course," Dante stalled, while he tried to come up with the best way to describe his role at the establishment. "I am responsible for everything that goes on here. I choose the wines and set the prices, and I've come to be a fixture in this beautiful tasting room. People come from…"

"...everywhere to see you, right Dante?" The voice was that of the owner, Alessandra, who walked up behind him and had long ago become familiar with Dante's boasts and his way of usurping her true ownership of Il Bar Spiriti.

"Si, signora, of course they do. But it is because you have made Bar Spiriti the best place in Sinalunga for a thirsty person to visit."

Both owner and employee exchanged slight smiles and Dante returned to his station while Alessandra poured more Prosecco into the ladies' flutes.

"Nicely done, Romeo," chuckled Paolo.

"Why didn't you warn me she was there," said Dante, only a little hurt but more perturbed that his romantic efforts had been thwarted.

"How? By throwing a cork at you? Or maybe this bottle," Paolo said, hefting the half-emptied bottle of Chianti. He used the gesture for his own benefit, tipping the bottle to the side and pouring a glass of the wine while Alessandra's attention was elsewhere.

Dante pouted and leaned on the bar to await another opportunity. He picked up the drying towel, spun it from hand to hand, and watched Alessandra tend to "his" customers. He liked his boss and got along well enough, and she let him have a bit of freedom in her dining room. But only a bit.

Alessandra left the table and wagged a finger at him, but her smile revealed that she expected this behavior from Dante, and with his good looks and charm she probably assumed he added something to the atmosphere of the room anyway.

"So," Dante said to Paolo, "you're going to Genoa in two days?"

"Si, on Friday. Why?"

"You've never worked anywhere but in your father's vineyard. Surely, sitting here drinking our wine hasn't taught you anything about working in a restaurant, and you can't expect Zia Rita to waste time teaching you."

"What do you have in mind," Paolo asked.

Dante threw the towel in Paolo's face and grinned.

"I have in mind that you learn something about waiting tables and pouring wine, right here, before you leave. You can help me tonight and tomorrow, and 'learn the ropes,' as they say in America."

The reference stung a bit, because Paolo knew that he had once before described his true travel wishes to Dante, but he shrugged it off, swung the towel over his shoulder, and stepped off the stool. He turned immediately in the direction of the table with the two young women, but Dante cut him off.

"Sorry, amico, they've already been served," and pointed his friend in the direction of the table with middle-aged parents and three school-aged children.

6

MODANE, FRANCE

*H*e paced the room distractedly, pulling his cell phone out of the jacket pocket to check for messages, then jammed it back in place, irritated that she hadn't called yet.

His face was stern and unwrinkled, his black hair combed straight back from his forehead, and he carried himself with the confident air of someone both experienced and street-smart. He reached up to scratch his cheek with his left hand, a hand with smooth unblemished skin, mismatched against his mottled right hand scarred from the fire that exploded in his fist on his last mission.

A plan to smuggle truffles was too far-fetched to believe. Which is exactly why he liked the idea so much, and why he believed the plot couldn't fail.

"It would work," he concluded, "smuggling precious cargo." He smiled at the mere thought of it.

It would take more than one person, but best not to involve more than himself and one other. He knew a most devious woman, one so treacherous that he had trouble trusting her himself. In fact, he didn't trust her. Criminals had a different notion of trust that wouldn't equate to what civilized society considered for the word.

"You rely on someone," he thought to himself, "and reliance only lasts as long as the job does. Never trust."

But he had to admit that his accomplice was scary by any measure.

They talked about the plan for weeks, considered every possible angle, listed every possible weakness. Soon, they were both convinced that it would work, even with all the fakes and counterfakes that would be required.

"Don't worry," she said, in a sonorous voice that seemed a pitch too low for a woman. "They'll never figure out what we're after until it's over."

No killing, she said, as if to reassure him about a question he had never asked. In his past experience of working with her, he had heard lots of nasty stories but never got any hint that people had died at her command. Still, the cold, black look in her eyes unsettled him, and he had to wonder how much he didn't know.

"We're in it for the money," he kept repeating, "that was clear. There's lots of money to be had from smuggling. And this – well, this will make us rich."

There were a few complications, but he was sure they could iron them out. "We're in it for the money," he said again. If she was willing, he would be too.

So they met in Modane one last time before going their separate ways. They ate and drank, he subconsciously raising the wine glass with his left hand to keep his blotchy right hand from view. They repeated every step of the process, until they had memorized their roles. Then she kissed him good night – it felt a bit perfunctory this time – and they parted.

She insisted on staying in separate hotels during this time in Modane. "We don't want anyone to be able to develop suspicions," she said in her resonant voice. She could be very firm and, in this case, he knew she wouldn't reconsider.

Besides, he had things to do too. He had to arrange the truck, set up rendezvous points, talk to the people along the way they would need to work with, and find a truffle hunter who would not be smart enough to be suspicious.

"What about the police at the border? Should I bribe them?" he asked.

"No, you idiot. If you bribe them now, they'll have time to re-consider. We'll deal with them when the time comes."

Her flare-ups were not that common, especially before a job began; she seemed to understand the importance of maintaining a respectful working relationship. But she would occasionally snap, as she had this time, and he accepted it. The steely glint in her eyes made him worry.

7

TIME TO GO

*H*e woke up early the next morning. He could tell it was a combination of excitement and fear. Not fear in the usual sense. He had accepted difficult assignments before and survived, but every new exploit carried its own risks.

While he sat with his coffee in the hotel lobby that morning, it occurred to him that he was more afraid of her than of failing.

"We've worked together before," he thought, "and I should feel at ease by now." But there was something in her eye, in the way she looked over her shoulder at him that gave him the creeps.

"She said we couldn't meet." It made sense, but he called her on the cell phone anyway to make sure they were ready to go.

"I am," she said, "Are you?" An octave lower, full of questioning suspicion.

"Yes," he assured her, taking slight umbrage at her undisguised doubt. And they hung up.

He was taking the car to the drop off location, then hitching a ride the rest of the way. She drove ahead in her own car. But that was fine with him. He didn't want to trust her with the details of the drop-off. As he thought that, he had to wonder whether he liked this task more because it would give him the slightest bit of power over her.

"Stupid," he called myself after the thought. She would not have agreed to something that didn't keep her in command.

So they both started off, at different times and along different roads, both ending up in Alba later in the day.

They set up in the little town as the streets buzzed with the seasonal influx of tourists. He knew she had been going to Alba for a few days at a time for the last couple months. He knew she had a boyfriend there; she had to. That was part of the plan.

"He has to trust me," she told her collaborator at the time. He almost laughed; after all this time together, he had trouble trusting her; but she was adept at using guile to draw an unwary man into her plot.

With the streets of Alba crowded with the truffle-hungry tourists at this time of year, the would-be smugglers expected the crowds to help them to remain inconspicuous.

"We'll probably see each other in a while," he suggested, "right?"

"Are you kidding?" she said. "In Alba is where I set the bait. I can't be seen with you."

"Okay," he reminded himself, "we're in this for the money."

8

BRINGING EVIL TO ALBA

*S*haking hands required a man to offer his right, even the ugly scarred appendage that he was left to carry around with him. So he reached out to the farmer and shook his hand with an air of nonchalance and confidence.

He had checked on this farmer earlier, before traveling here from Modane. The farmer was a truffle hunter, and he had innocently accepted the hired task, making plans in advance of the smugglers' arrival.

"Digging for truffles is a delicate business," said the trifolào, with hand gestures to illustrate his point that the unearthed gems be treated with great care. "Scratching or cutting the surface reduces the value of the find. You use a zappino to gently lift the truffle from the earth."

"A zappino is a small pick," he continued, chuckling at the confused look on his guest's face, then he handed over the little tool.

That laugh made the smuggler mad. "You'll not be needed much longer," he thought, casting a malicious gaze upon his host. He hefted the zappino in his hand. It felt good, strong enough and just the right length. It could be used as a weapon.

The old farmer's look turned gray then, and his brow knitted together in one long V-shaped furrow.

"What is it?" asked the visitor.

Without lifting his head, the old guy dusted the ground with his toe and peered upward at his guest so that the pupils of his eyes were lightly shrouded by the downcast eyelashes.

"Claudio died yesterday. He was a good friend and a skilled truffle hunter." He paused and looked at the zappino.

"They found his body in the field," he continued, "where his dogs had laid down beside him." With a tremor of suspicion in his voice, he added, "They said he must have tripped on the roots of the tree, and..." pausing to look at the digging tool once more... "he fell onto his zappino.

"That's pazzo!" the farmer said, "crazy. Claudio could not have done that."

The old guy didn't have to spell it out. Seeing the sharpened pick in the smuggler's hand, he felt a hint of concern, as he would suspect any outsider when a friend was recently killed.

The farmer was left to brood for his lost friend as the man returned to his rental car and drove down the road to Alba. Returning to the festive mood of the village and the street parties that claimed the night, the smuggler spied his accomplice on the next block. She was talking to a young couple and laughing it up. By their hand signals he could tell she was asking for directions.

"Funny how she can turn off the evil in her eyes," he thought, "and turn gracious and almost girlishly shy when it suits her."

She had a look that lit up her face. Her eyes sparkled, her cheeks swelled with a broad smile, even the freedom of her gestures described someone who was happy and excited about being here in Alba, knowing no one, and interacting with strangers easier than she interacted with her partner in crime. It was a great act.

At that moment he wondered whether he was just a pawn she was using to complete this deal. A needed partner to finish off details that she, along, couldn't do.

They were standing only about twenty feet apart – he assumed that distance would be enough. Just as she was signing off with that couple, she looked at him and winked. She had known he was there the whole time and didn't say anything. Of course.

That wink reassured him and he settled down. It wasn't just the wink, it was the impish smile on her face that won him over.

The other couple turned to leave and he contemplated going up to her and pretending to be flirting, just a guy on the street in Alba, in search of a girl. But she used the slightest side-to-side motion of her head and a subtle flick of her fingers hanging down by her hip to warn him not to try.

His thoughts drifted to Claudio, with a zappino sticking out from between his ribs.

"We're in it for the money," her gesture said. "No killing." But he wondered about the dead farmer.

9

NO COMPROMISE

*T*he next morning he returned to the farm to continue to develop his relationship with the trifolào. The truffle harvest had just begun, but it was slight; the real crop wouldn't be coming in for a couple of weeks. Just enough time for the smugglers to launch their plan.

"The truffle hunter I hired – stupid man," he thought to himself driving up the dirt-rutted lane, "has already taught me all that I need to know. Today, we'll be out in his fields testing my abilities."

"You know, we won't be searching for truffles in the daytime, not really," the farmer said.

The visitor didn't really intend to search for truffles with the trifolào, anyway. He had promised to help the farmer find a new *market for his truffles, a promise that encouraged the farmer to teach the methods and share the crop.*

"We can harvest more truffles," the thief added, a further enticement, "then we can deliver them to market and split the profits." Or so he said.

The farmer was one of the new breed of trifolài, a bit outside the fraternity of truffle hunters, someone who would rather make money than preserve the tradition of the specialty. He was the perfect target for the smuggler.

"Today, we're just practicing," he told the farmer. And that was true, but the visitor wondered for a moment how few things he said anymore that were true.

"But if I'm going to help you find more truffles, I need to know how to get to them without damaging our crop." He fingered the zappino and imagined plunging it into more than the earth.

They practiced on trees near the farmhouse, the trifolào didn't want to wander into the fields in daylight and expose the location of his truffle fields to prying eyes. After an hour, they returned to the farmhouse. The farmer was warming up to this stranger and asked him in for a quick meal but he declined.

"I need to return to Alba," he said, "to make arrangements for the sale." Another lie.

The farmer's dog was not as trusting as his owner and seemed to sense a certain wickedness in this visitor. The dog knew the man, but was beginning to act suspicious around him.

10

PORT OF TRIPOLI, LIBYA

Two men sat close together at a table beside the docks in the Port of Tripoli. Each had a tendency to seize his cup of coffee like a bear seizes her cub; not with fingers on the handle but by palming the ceramic vessel and wrapping his thick fingers around it.

Their conversation went in spurts, several comments exchanged in seconds, terse words with few syllables, followed by long moments of silence. Both were grizzled and muscular, although the attractive muscles of youth were now shrouded by the folds of midlife's layers.

One wore a close-fitting flannel hat; the other wore a stocking cap familiar to men who spent their lives on the sea. Both were veterans of hard times and knew not to turn down money where it could be found.

"We're to sail up to Genoa, without stopping at ports along the way. The port there is so busy that the masters can't keep up with boats that tie down along the quay."

"Okay. Then what?" asked the other.

"Find a truck," said the first. "Nothing showy, gotta be inconspicuous. Can't steal it, have to buy it so no one's gonna be looking for it for a while."

"Whose money?" asked the second.

"Ours." The first man paused, recognizing the doubt in his partner's voice. "I've worked with her before. She'll pay."

They sat for long moments after that, sipping their coffee and staring out at the ships they once dreamed would be their ticket to adventure. That was when both were young and foolish. Now they were old and broke. The sea took their youth, stole their families, and left them with empty dreams.

The first man put down his cup with a clunk, indicating that it was empty and he was done. Before he could rise from the table, the second had one more question.

"How much is it worth?"

"More than you've made in the last five years," came the very simple answer.

11

WAKING LATE

The work had been nearly completed among the vines. Paolo slept later than usual, mostly to his father's disappointment. Dito was too old to remember that a young man needed, or wanted, more sleep. Especially in the morning with a slight chill in the air. That made it so much better to roll over in bed and sleep until noon.

Dito had worked hard most of his life. His father had been gruff with him just as he was with Paolo. But, with his own years multiplying, Dito decided that his own father was right. Sleep is necessary, but a man was supposed to get up with the sun and be productive.

So when he passed his son's bedroom door he glanced in. With a slight hesitation in his step, Dito moved on. It was not an argument that a father won with a son. Besides, Dito said to himself, soon Paolo would be gone and – at this he looked down at his feet – maybe not return.

"*Non capisco*," he mumbled to himself. "I don't understand."

Later in the morning, when Dito was already out in the barn, Paolo stumbled into his mother's kitchen. Catrina was done cooking breakfast, and she wagged her finger at her son for his long hours in bed, but otherwise didn't upbraid him.

"It's midday," she said, a chiding remark said with a mother's smile. "What would your father think?"

Paolo knew what his father would think. But what was the point? They worked sunrise to sunset during the growing season, and even longer during the harvest. Now that the season was over and there was nothing to do, why get up early?

"What does papa do in that barn, anyway?" he asked.

"He does what he has to do. He keeps busy," was her reply.

"But what does he have to do?"

Catrina's look was a mixture of patience and love. "He has to keep busy."

12

CAFFÉ ROSSETTI

There was an upside to not being together in Alba. She was always telling him not to drink so much wine.

"It'll blur your judgment," she said.

"Like choosing you for a partner," he almost blurted out one night.

In Alba, the birthplace of Barolo and other magnificent Italian wines, not partaking of the vinous treasures would have been a sin. Red wine, white wine, even many sparkling wines made from Cortese and Moscato. He couldn't drink them all, but he didn't mind making a serious go of it.

So he found a shady seat on the sidewalk outside of Caffé Rossetti, and relaxed. Piazza Rossetti itself was small and just off the main pedestrian thoroughfare, so he didn't think he'd run into anyone that he didn't want to see. Like his accomplice, or the truffle hunter he hired.

But the piazza still had the glow of the Old World: young girls in their pretty dresses, young men following close behind, mamas and papas with younger kids in tow. Old men gathered at café tables and arguing about the latest soccer score. It was easy to settle in and just watch the world go by.

Alba was growing on him.

"I had never been to Alba before we hatched this plan," he thought, but he intended to return when it was over – with the millions of euros that he expected to have then.

But she didn't want that. She said a smart criminal never returns to the scene of the crime. A smart criminal.

"And we're in it for the money," he repeated to himself, once again.

13

ERASE THE COMPLICATIONS

*A*fter sating himself on food and wine at Caffè Rossetti, the man returned to the farm the next day, and the dog's natural suspicions were once again on display.

"The dog knew me," he thought "and acted suspicious as soon as I got out of my car."

"Hello," the hunter waved at him as he walked from his barn. He seemed full of spirit that day. Apparently, he was in it for the money too.

"Hello. What is the plan for this morning?" the visitor asked.

The trifolào said they had been practicing under hazelnut trees, and there would be some truffles there. But now he said that *his best crop comes from the oak trees on the northern part of his farm.*

"I couldn't care less where he got his truffles from," the smuggler thought to himself. "He still thinks I'm here to get his truffles." Then it occurred to him that, when the farmer was gone, why shouldn't the visitor take the crop too?

Later that day he called her on the phone. She told him that she had set everything up. It was easy, she said, and he could hear the sound of feminine pride in her voice: She had fooled another man. He wondered how many men she had fooled - - whether she was just fooling him.

They talked about the next steps. Since she was ready and he had honed the hunting skills, they didn't need the hunter any more.

"I can't dig up enough truffles by myself," he said, reminding her of his earlier concern about this.

She said she knew how to do it. He knew she had spent time in Alba before, but he didn't realize that this time included practicing truffle hunting.

"Work at night, sleep during the day," was what she said.

They could share the locations, he said, split them up and get more done.

"It's the only way," she said.

That evening, he returned to the farm. This time, the dog snarled and made him nervous.

He walked resolutely toward the barn, trying to convince the dog that he belonged there, and not to growl and bite him, but he made the man nervous. The farmer was not in the barn, but the dog followed the visitor in, just steps behind.

As he passed through the wide open doors of the barn, he looked up and saw a short metal bar, some piece of farm machinery, no doubt. He turned and glanced briefly at the dog, reached up to grab the bar, and spun around before the animal could react. The bar came right down on the dog's head.

There was a whimper, then a sound that sounded like "harrumph," as the animal dropped to the earth. It was like the dog was getting in the last word. Well, it was his last word.

The man knew he had to reach the farmer before he came into the barn; if he saw the dog like this, the next step would be much more difficult.

He walked out of the barn, looking both ways before crossing to his car to retrieve the shovel. When he turned around, he saw that the farmer was already there, he was already walking into the barn. The visitor still had the metal bar in his hand.

He walked up behind the trifolào and saw that the farmer was standing there staring down at his lifeless dog. His arms were slightly spread, palms up, as if to say, "What's this?"

"That's appropriate," the visitor thought, that they would both die together. He swung the blunt weapon down in a swift arc on the man's head.

"Didn't feel a thing," the scoundrel told himself.

He returned to his car to get the shovel. Now he had to bury the dog and the man.

The two smugglers began hunting truffles in earnest that night. They had to get out there before full night fell, because the trifolài would come in the early morning hours. They didn't need dogs or pigs; she had already stolen the program from her boy-friend that mapped out all the best truffle-hunting grounds.

When the man unearthed his first truffle, he brought it to his nose.

"What a scent!" he exclaimed, "It was everything those boring foodies kept yammering about back at the restaurant."

He was amazed and, at the same time, converted, and de-cided that he would save some of these and treat himself after they had smuggled the mother lode.

14

GENOA

The Genovese know their food. In a land such as Italy, where even peasants enjoyed an almost unfair portion of great meals, the Genovese believed they stood out.

And so it was that Rita and Stefano had such a following. Their restaurant on Via del Mare offered a broad range of dishes from the Ligurian region, but generously included specialties from up and down the Italian peninsula. Seafood dominated, but they also included Florentine sauces, Umbrian beef, Calabrian shellfish, myriad seafood delicacies from the Adriatic, and borderline-Austrian/ German accents from the Tyrolean border on the north.

They shared cooking responsibilities and, while Stefano was the workhorse in the kitchen, Rita was the genius behind their menu. She could taste a dish and pick out all the ingredients, arranging them in order of quantity and even the time the ingredients were added to the pan. With Rita's uncanny sense of smell, Stefano wondered at times whether it was a distraction. When they walked through the market together before opening each day, he feared she would be overwhelmed and go a bit crazy.

Quite the opposite happened. Rita combined her sense of smell with her mental checklist of what she wanted for that day. Striding purposefully between the stalls with heavy smells of fresh fish, delicate aromas of herbs, and pungent odors of cheese, Rita would sometimes veer suddenly to one side and point right at the thing she was looking for.

"What a sense of direction," Stefano laughed, "and what a sense of purpose!"

They stocked their pantry with eclectic items but managed to reserve space for foodstuffs that were true to the Ligurian menu. It was this approach that made Ristorante Girasole so popular with the locals.

And locals were their main stock in trade. They wouldn't mind having more tourists to drop in but, truth be told, the dining room probably couldn't hold them. As it was, the tables were full from the opening bell until lights out, making each evening an exhausting event and leaving Rita and Stefano, and their help, anxious to sit for a spell and nibble at their own dinner late after closing.

15

OLD SEAMEN JOIN THE PLOT

The two old seamen shed some of their somber persona once they pushed off from the dock at Tripoli. No one would describe them as happy or even content; but the sound of waves lapping up on the hull of their boat soothed each man in a way that the same waves up on the dock could not have done.

They were not men of words, personality traits that served many sailors well for long sea voyages. A talkative man on deck was usually considered a nuisance. It was like being seated next to a stranger on a plane who insisted on talking rather than letting you read your book. The sailor, like the stranger, was too close for comfort and nothing short of violence could shut him up.

So these men did their work and otherwise kept to themselves.

They had known each other since their school days; it would be too much to say they had been friends. But they both loved the sea and both had the same unrealistic dreams of what it would do for them. So they understood each other very well.

They spoke only when directions or actions were required, and when they sat in the galley to have a meal and drink tumblers of the clear, strong, alcohol that the Libyan people had tried to abolish, but failed.

"What do we do when we get the truck?" asked the man with the ever-present stocking cap.

"She said to move all our cargo into the truck and head for Alba. I'm supposed to call her once we're on the road."

"What about the boat?"

"I know an inlet just east of the port of Genoa that shelters many of the fishing boats. Ours is a fishing boat so it won't be noticed if we leave it there for a few days."

The man in the stocking cap looked at the other one with some skepticism.

"Locals notice everything," was all he said.

"That's right. Which is why I bought this boat from one of them a few months ago. They'll see it and recognize it, so it'll take a while to realize that it doesn't belong. By then, we'll be gone."

The second didn't smile often, and even this statement didn't make his lips curl, but he looked back at his tumbler, gave it a long slurp, and grunted with satisfaction.

16

TOO MANY TRUFFLES

*W*ork at night, sleep during the day.

That's what the smugglers did for several nights running. Most truffle hunters would work a few hours just before dawn, but these two were working from the minute the sun set through until about two in the morning, leaving the fields only because they expected the trifolài to be coming out at any moment.

The haul was significant. On the first night they realized that the plan needed a new step. They couldn't hide these truffles in their hotel rooms; the strong aromas would easily attract unwanted questions.

"Don't worry," she said. She told him to put them in a sack among this stand of trees, cover the sack with dried and decaying leaves, and she would get back to him later in the day.

Ah, day. Time to sleep.

He went straight away to the Hotel Savoy, stripped and stood for twenty minutes in a hot shower to cast the night chill from his bones, then he sought the comfort of his bed. He didn't recall whether the sheets were cold; he was asleep before the thought would register.

It seemed only minutes later — probably hours, the way sleep plays with our memory — that his cell phone rang.

"I have a warehouse we can store them in," she said. "The location is written on a slip of paper that I put on the sack of truffles."

He was still sleepy but realized quickly that she wouldn't have simply brought the paper to him. It was daylight and we couldn't be seen together. He started feeling like a vampire.

He rose reluctantly from bed and checked the time. It had indeed been a couple of hours, not minutes. But, still, a couple hours sleep is not enough!

He did as he was instructed. He knew he'd have to cover his actions somewhat because he could be seen now. But the sack was concealed far away from the truffle fields and he expected that most people would be about their business now.

The slip of paper gave directions, but also provided a series of numbers: 18-45-23-41. This must a combination, he thought, probably to the warehouse. It was. So then at the end of every long night spent in the fields, he had the additional task of driving the truffles out of town to this warehouse.

"Could you drive them tonight?" he asked.

"That would call attention to us," she responded. "If we are both seen at the warehouse, people will think there's something suspicious. You, you look like a farmer and this is a farmer's warehouse. People will just think you work for him and you're delivering his vegetables before going to market."

17

THE PORT OF GENOA

The sailors timed their arrival in Genoa to dock in the mid-morning hours. This gave them two advantages: It was the time many fishermen arrived with their catch and the port master would be up to his gills in arriving boats. It also allowed them enough daylight hours to find a truck, load it with their cargo, and relocate the boat. Afterward, they would drive north and disappear on the country roads of Liguria.

They motored quietly into one of the busy parts of the Genovese port. The first man's hand was at the wheel, and he knew the best place to hide was in plain sight. He never wavered and didn't scan the port with his eyes. He knew where he was going and he didn't want to attract attention by indecision.

His partner on board was preparing the cargo. They wanted to tie up, produce their counterfeit passes and fake documents, register with the master on duty, and go get some food on shore. They knew the port master wouldn't have the boat listed. They were delivering the day's catch of shrimp and eel; neither was interesting enough to be weighed and surveyed by the authorities. And their paperwork was very convincing. With all the demands on the master's time, their boat wouldn't be searched until late evening, when it would already be empty.

Empty, that is, except for the trails of shrimp and eel that they purchased along the way to stink up the hold.

Their meal was short, utilitarian, and gruff, like the men who consumed it. They didn't exchange a word the whole time; a restaurant table was no place to talk about their current plan, and they didn't have anything else in common that would produce a conversation of another sort.

They paid their bill and walked out of the restaurant onto the streets of Genoa.

The first man put on a barely more convivial tone when he questioned locals about where they might be able to buy a truck.

"We're new to Genoa and want to set up a ceramics import business here."

The ploy was weak, but no one questioned it. They got some suggestions and a couple of brush-offs, and the second man had to restrain himself from flipping these rude people the finger.

By mid-afternoon, they had visited three truck lots. They had selected the truck they needed at the first one, but wanted to lower the possible suspicion by seeming too anxious. In the end, they simply returned to the first lot where the salesman was very eager for the sale and wouldn't be suspicious of their motives.

They drove the truck back to the quay and unloaded their cargo. The second man drove away to their rendez-vous point while the first man piloted the boat to the hidden fishing port he described earlier.

They were on the road in time to have dinner in Asti, a half-hour drive from Alba, where they would wait for instructions from the lady.

The ride through Ligurian hills, merging into the Piedmont – literally, the "foot of the mountains" – further north, was a pleasant one, but held little interest for these wizened sailors. These men were drawn to the sea and the feel of a boat swaying under their feet, so the green hills and black asphalt, and the thud-thud of tires over the roadway held little interest for them.

They arrived at the outskirts of Asti and randomly settled on a little hole-in-wall restaurant for some dinner. The first man flipped open his cell phone, dialed a number quickly, and had to wait only two rings before a woman's voice came on the line.

"Are you there?"

"Yes, we're outside Asti."

"Take A33 south toward Alba. There's a little town called Barraccone on the north side of the roadway. Turn right onto SS231 and go to the Hotel Vecchio. There's a room for you under the name of Santino. There's also a note left for you, describing a place to park the truck. Stay there until further notice. I'll be in touch."

18

ON THE TRAIN TO GENOA

Morning came early in farm country, especially on this particular day for Paolo who was eager to head to the train station and board for Genoa. The late-September air was cool and fresh, let in liberally by bedroom windows that were left open at this time of year. There were fewer human sounds – no pickers or vineyard equipment humming in the distance – but the music of farm creatures and birds still wafted in through his window. Paolo finished packing almost mechanically, with one ear tuned to the sounds of his farming life, but his mind fixed on the trip ahead.

Most of his clothes and other things he had arranged the night before in anticipation of *questo gran gita,* "this grand trip," so Paolo could take time to enjoy *la prima colazione,* the brief first meal of the day, from Catrina's kitchen. *Secondo colazione* would be bigger and was generally taken at around ten o'clock when most Italians wanted a brief respite from the day's activities. By that time, Paolo would already be at the train station. But for a little while, at least, Paolo lingered over his mother's fresh rolls and bowls of fruit, then sliced liberally through the hunks of cheese that served to complete the meal.

Paolo returned to his upstairs bedroom and, from the balcony outside his room on the second floor, he stood to enjoy a last sip of espresso and stared off into the distance. He was surprised when a touch of melancholy took him unawares, and tried to shrug it off. Peering beyond the rooftops of *pietra cotta*, the baked stone tiles of the houses that surrounded the dell'Uco home, he could see farmland and rows of vines that stretched off into the distance. He wondered how many families had shared the land he gazed upon, and how many centuries these farms had provided sustenance to the people in the houses that now were slowly coming to life in the cool morning air. His second thoughts were fleeting, though, and he quickly downed the last swallow of espresso when thoughts of Genoa surged back into his mind.

Trooping down the stairs he gave his mother a thoughtful hug, then stepped out into the still-cool sunshine where his father was waiting for him next to the truck. Looking at his mother's little garden, then at the dusty cobble-stoned road at his feet, Paolo wondered again what his father saw in the parched earth of this farm, but his thoughts were distracted by the sight of a glimmering tear that Dito tried unsuccessfully to hold back. Dito looked down and brushed his toes against the stones, then turned to climb into the driver's seat.

Catrina stepped out through the doorway, prepared for this moment. She quickly hugged her son again, spun him around, and told him to go.

Paolo threw his bags into the back of the truck and climbed into the seat next to his silent and sullen father. Dito cranked the engine which started with a grudge, and they wheeled off in the direction of Arezzo, the nearest train station and about an hour drive along country roads.

Both men stared blankly through the dirty windshield, without speaking a word until Dito swung the truck into the driveway in front of the train station. With his fingers on the door handle, Paolo looked over at his father and offered a slight smile.

"I'll be back in a few weeks," Paolo said, then he looked down at the floorboards when he realized he had already lengthened the "one week, maybe two" promise he made two nights earlier at the dinner table.

Dito's head turned in Paolo's direction but cocked to the side. He face was drawn and a little sad, revealing that he thought this trip was just the first of many, but he held the gaze for a bit until his son looked back toward him.

"*Ritorna a la casa, subito*," he said while extending his hand. "Come home, soon." Paolo took his father's leathery hand, shook it once and let go. Before either man could see a tear drop, Paolo pulled the door handle up with a jerk, and swung his legs out onto the pavement.

"Ciao, papa," he said, and turned to enter the train station.

The train station in Arezzo is small in comparison to other Italian *ferroviarie*, the network of rail depots that serve the entire peninsula. The stations in Rome, Venice, Milan, and Naples serve as commercial hubs of those cities and include many adjacent hotels and shops; Arezzo's station located on the Piazza della Repubblica is smaller and exists mainly for its role in transportation, unheralded as a "destination" in itself.

Paolo stepped up to the window, exchanged the common pleasantries with the clerk, and bought a ticket to Genoa, known as Genova to Italians. For a brief moment – and with a wry shrug – he wondered why he was buying a round-trip ticket. Tapping the little piece of paper on his outstretched fingers, Paolo quickly chased that thought and swore to honor his promise to return to his parents. It was a thought that would impose itself on his mind more often in the coming days.

The clerk pointed Paolo in the direction of *binario 3,* the railside where his train would be waiting. *La prima classe* was for tourists with too much money to burn; Paolo was satisfied with the accommodations in *la seconda classe,* where he settled into a window seat and waited for the departure. The train's furnishings were comfortable, if not luxurious. The seats were cushioned and most could be stretched out to meet the seat directly across, forming a bed for overnight travel. There were racks above for one's *bagagli,* luggage, and the window would open by sliding the panes across. Paolo did this, in part to look out on the train station of his local region, in part to revel in the excitement of a trip alone, and in part to get a better look at the pretty *ragazze* who were also boarding the train.

Staring out at the scene from the window, he realized that the parting at truckside had distracted him and he forgot to buy provisions for the train ride. Vendors hawked their food and beverages on the *binarii* between each departing train, pleased to sell their sandwiches, sodas, wine, and water to the travelers before the train pulled out of the station.

Paolo opened the window and whistled for one of the cart minders to come over. He bought a bottle of water, a bottle of wine, and two sandwiches. The journey to Genoa would take just over four hours and he wanted ample sustenance, even though it couldn't match the food at his mother's table.

He settled in and waited for the sounds of departure. With a whistle and the hiss of brakes being released, the train lurched forward and began the slow process of acceleration. More whistles, the metallic ring of wheels turning on iron rails, and the sounds of the city washed together in an urban cacophony that Paolo loved. It was vibrant, unlike the quiet stillness of the countryside, and Paolo breathed deeply in the knowledge that he was now on his way.

The train left the station at about ten o'clock in the morning, stopping just before noon in Florence and picking up and dropping off some of its passengers. At the appointed departure time, groaning wheels once again announced the time had come to head for another city, Pisa, and the train began its next leg of the journey. Paolo reservedly sipped at his water, knowing that this bottle was as precious as the ubiquitous wine, and he ate one of the two sandwiches before the train arrived at Pisa Centrale.

Larger than the humble train station in Arezzo, Pisa's building is one of the most beautiful in the city. Damaged during World War II, its 19th century façade was restored and stands now as a testament to Italians perseverance during wars between invading armies.

The stop lasted about thirty minutes, time enough for Paolo to stretch his legs and wander out onto the *binario* and buy another bottle of water. He didn't want to leave the platform, fearing that a sudden departure – Italian trains were still notoriously unpredictable – would leave him stranded longer than he planned in Pisa.

"I will return to Pisa again," he promised himself silently. "And climb the great tower."

The next leg of the trip took him to his destination, Genoa, first passing through more of Italy's idyllic countryside. It was a transformative experience to come from the country's inner regions like Tuscany with its green rolling hills, orchards, and vineyards and travel to the coastal regions like Liguria, with its endless miles of beach and rocky coastline. Paolo had modest experience with travel and wasn't a stranger to Italy's shores, but he had not yet seen such wondrous places as the Amalfi coast, the Adriatic seashore, Taormina in Sicily, or the Cinque Terre. He had been to Genoa when he was younger, and was most familiar with Liguria, so he contented himself with the opportunity to return there.

"I will see all of Italy, then all of the world," was another promise he made himself.

19

CITY OF SHIPS

T he train's speed slacked as it moved into the maze of tracks entering Genoa Piazza Principe, the city's train station on Piazza Acquaverde. With a huff and the grinding of metallic brakes, the cars came to a halt beside the *binario* and Paolo grabbed his bag and stepped quickly onto the platform, and into the bustle and noise of this city.

He made his way out of the train station and stood on a corner, looking very much like a tourist with his bag in hand and slightly lost appearance. He turned slowly to take in his surroundings, not in confusion but to absorb every moment of his return to the City of Ships. It was a nickname he bestowed on it when he was a boy, a boy mesmerized by the ancient history of shipbuilding in Genoa, as well as its continuing role in world maritime commerce. Paolo's mother was right that he was suffering from a bit of wanderlust, but she thought the feeling had only just set in. Paolo knew that he had wanted to travel the world, preferably by ship, since he was five years old.

The city's true nickname was *La Superba*, a moniker that honors its wondrous past and wealth of monuments. For centuries, it was the stepping off point for great expeditions, the birthplace of Christopher Columbus, and no doubt the splendor of sailing ships were inspiration for Columbus' early dreams of exploration.

It was a typical port and seaside city, with most of the avenues running parallel to the Mediterranean Sea that Genoa spreads its arms around. The city had over 1,000 years of seafaring history, served as a major trading port of the Ligurian region, and so it had many layers of streets that backed up the shoreline and climbed the rambling hills of the coastline. Genovese grumbled that too many years had cast too many problems on them and their home, but few could bring themselves to leave the city.

Paolo stood still for a moment and gathered his thoughts about direction. He knew that Ristorante Girasole was on Via del Mare, but he had not been there and certainly not without an adult's hand to hold, so steering himself in the proper direction would be a challenge.

"*Scusi, signore, puo dirmi dov'é la Via del Mare?*" he asked a stranger. The gray-haired man was standing on the corner, reading *Il Giornale,* and looked up at the taller Paolo for a moment before responding. He added the formality of a chin-rub, a quick arching of eyebrows, and then peered back at his questioner.

"*Questa via,*" he said, this way, pointing to his right, then offered a few more turns and suggestions, even throwing in an unsolicited recommendation for a wonderful café known for *un ristretto* caffé, a particularly strong mini-cup of espresso known in the city, then finished his commentary by saying, "*e' giusto li,*" "it's right there."

Paolo thanked him and went on his way, smiling at the friendly greeting. He even decided to take the man up on his recommendation for *un ristretto* caffé.

The short walk to Via del Mare gave Paolo a chance to see and smell the city. In fact, the smells of cities, particularly those in Europe and other very old metropolises, revealed much about their character. A denizen of the farms, Paolo didn't have much of an inventory of olfactory memories to make of the smells around him that day, but he always marveled at how old cities mingled food, wine, coffee, car exhaust, and manufacturing smells into some kind of symphony. It was not always pleasant, but no newly constructed concrete-and-steel urban setting could cast such a spell on a person. This was what greeted Paolo as he walked down the streets of Genoa in search of his aunt's restaurant.

20

RISTORANTE GIRASOLE

Stepping off the curb at Via del Mare, Paolo walked into Ristorante Girasole about half past eight, just as the dinner rush was filling the dining room. Stepping through the narrow doorway into the semi-lighted room, he was enveloped with the aromas of the Ligurian coast, and the chatter and clatter of a typical Italian dining room. He let his eyes adjust to the difference in light, let his ears adjust to the din around him, and gazed across the room toward the kitchen, then to the slender man circling the tables with practiced grace.

Paolo stood at the door and waited, bag in hand, but probably looked more like a guest waiting to be seated than a family member on a visit. Finally, the dining room manager spun past one more table and approached him.

It was Stefano, his aunt's husband, and he briefly took Paolo for nothing more than the dinner guest he seemed to be.

"Uno?" Stefano asked, casting his arm wide toward the dining room. Following his own arm, Stefano's eyes searched for an open table, then he paused and looked back over his shoulder.

"Paolo!?" He quickly furrowed his brow playfully hinting that he'd been deceived, then spun around to hug his nephew.

"*Che cos'è?*" he asked. "How's it going? Rita didn't tell me you were expected today."

"Well, no, I just…" Paolo replied when released from the bear hug. "It's nothing; I just came for a visit."

For a moment the two men stood in expectant silence, then Stefano slapped Paolo on the back, grabbed his bag and threw it behind the counter, then took his nephew by the elbow back into the kitchen.

As the double-swinging kitchen doors swung inward, Rita looked up and dropped her spatula and tongs. She swung around the corner of the stainless steel prep table and wrapped her nephew in her arms. Paolo was taller than his diminutive aunt, but Rita left no doubt about her command of the embrace.

She stepped back and, grabbing him at the elbows with extended arms, Rita surveyed her new charge.

"You've grown up, you're tall and muscular. Dito must be working you hard."

Paolo smiled and shrugged his shoulders, without responding. He didn't want to dissuade his aunt from complimenting him, but didn't want her to hold onto the image of him as a farmer either.

Rita reached over the counter, pulled a loaf of bread, aromatic and herb-scented right from the oven, and gave it to Paolo. He was ready to yank off a hunk and enjoy it, when Rita shook her finger at him.

"You're not here to eat, you're here to work." She tossed him an apron and told him to grab a knife and slice the bread, then put it in a basket for the table near the door.

"It's too busy right now to visit properly. We'll talk later." Leaving Paolo in Stefano's charge, Rita took her turn in the dining room – she and Stefano liked to work both the "front" and the "back" of the restaurant – to greet guests and take orders to be delivered to her husband and Paolo in the back.

Paolo was truly hungry after such a long day, but the pace of life in a restaurant kitchen quickly vanquished any

thoughts of a leisurely meal. He took up his first assignment and quickly followed additional instructions from
Stefano. In what passed for only a minute or two, he got
into the work – just as the kitchen door flew open and a
young woman barged into the prep area. She was spectac-
ularly beautiful, with green eyes and long raven hair that
tumbled down her back. She was not family, Paolo knew,
so her presence here suggested she was an employee.

"Ciao, I'm Nicola," she said, "who are you?" busily managing her own chores and showing little respect for hierar-
chy here in the kitchen.

Momentarily speechless, Paolo wished for the moment
that he had Dante's swift wit.

"Okay," Nicola threw in to fill the dead air, "I need
one order of Trenette al Pesto, Cima, and Burrida… and a
platter of antipasto di casa."

Paolo smiled, muttered something "bella!" just as
Nicola swung around and glided back out to the dining
room. Stefano heard Paolo's comment and smiled know-
ingly in return.

Stefano was familiar with the effect that Nicola had on
men and knew that Paolo was doubly confounded by the
list of these typically Ligurian dishes.

"We call her Nicki."

Continuing, Stefano explained, "Trenette al Pesto is one of Liguria's most famous dishes. Other people think they can make it but not the way we do," headded with evident pride.

"I'll make it," Stefano said, "but I could use your help with the Cima. I have to stuff the veal with eggs, peas, cheese, and marjoram. Perhaps you could chop the herbs for me," he said as he slid a branch of marjoram over to Paolo at the cutting board.

"And don't worry about the Burrida either. Rita started it hours ago, cutting and stewing a dozen fish and shellfish and herbs. Our customers call it "Burrida di Rita" since her version is known throughout Genoa, and she won't let anyone touch it." At that, Stefano laughed, and added, "When Rita decides the recipe is hers, leave it alone, that's all I can say."

The dining room was full at Ristorante Girasole, a common occurrence at most restaurants on weekend nights such as this one, but Rita and Stefano's establishment was very popular and busy nights stretched into the week as well. They focused on food that was typical Genovese fare, adding ingredients from nearby regions as appropriate for each dish.

The pace of restaurant work was unlike anything Paolo had experienced in the quiet solitude of the vines, and more rushed than he witnessed at Il Bar Spiriti in Sinalunga. He may have scoffed at restaurant work in earlier days, assuming confidently that work in the vineyard was infinitely more physically demanding, but responding to the demands of sometimes impatient guests put greater stress on the pattern of work than did grapes that – mostly – just hung quietly on the vine.

But it was also energizing, and he quickly learned to contribute. The hours swept by, the tables were filled, cleared, and filled again, then as midnight approached and the last guests lingered over espresso and biscotti del lagaccio, the sweet fennel-scented cookies known well in Liguria, Paolo was able to catch his breath and take in the expanse of the restaurant.

Later in the night, as kitchen work switched from preparation to clean-up, Paolo helped Rita and Stefano and Nicki work the dining room and tend to the remaining guests. After the last table had been cleared, Nicki brought the plates and glasses in for washing, all the while sensing that Paolo was watching her. This brought a satisfied smile to her lips; enjoying the attention of men was a familiar experience.

Stefano was stacking plates on the sideboard and shot a glance in Rita's direction, cocking his head in Paolo's direction and getting a knowing nod and raised eyebrows from Rita in return. Paolo was working hard but struggling to adapt to the pace in a restaurant kitchen, with its strange menu items and wordless signals between the others that had been honed over many nights of teamwork.

For her part, Nicki was well adapted to the routine. They had hired her a year earlier, a little concerned at the time that she may not be able to handle the long hours and physical nature of restaurant work that escaped the attention of most people who remained on the other side of the kitchen door. But she fit in nicely, worked hard, and had become a fixture in Ristorante Girasole, and a welcome sight to their male guests.

21

LATE NIGHT REPAST

When everything was cleaned and put away, Rita lit the gas burners and prepared a quick platter of Gasse, a butterfly-shaped pasta, and dressed it with artichokes, onions, and garlic, and a splash of white wine. Stefano arranged a platter of cheese and some slices of fresh vegetables that had been grilled and marinated in olive oil, thyme, and balsamic vinegar, left over from the night's dining room service.

Nicki took down four plates and four glasses and set the table in the back of the kitchen with these and the utensils they would use. The three experienced restaurateurs moved smoothly through the kitchen with well-practiced motions, without comment or verbal communication, as if they were actors in a silent play.

Paolo knew they were fixing their own dinner but got no direction from his aunt or uncle, so he went back to help Nicki with her chore. She accepted the assistance, occasionally pointing to another table article that she wanted Paolo to retrieve and set, then the four converged on their late night repast. Once the meal was set and all the food was delivered to the table, Rita, Nicki, and Paolo sat down, but Stefano went back into the closet for one more ingredient.

He returned with a bottle of Ceretto Barolo. Setting it carefully on the table, he pulled a *cavatappo*, corkscrew, from his back pocket and went to work on the willing cork. Paolo had seen many bottles opened and listened to the pop of many corks, and at first he shrugged off the ritual and focused his attention on the food at the table. But following the expected "pop," the room was immediately filled with a fragrance he was not accustomed to. Stefano poured a half glass of the deep red wine for everyone then set the bottle down in the middle of the table, within reach of each of them. This dinner was family style, where everyone was expected to help themselves to wine and food. Nobody got served back in the kitchen.

Paolo took a sip of the wine and paused. After letting the full body of the liquid glide down his throat, his mouth slowly opened as if he had something to say, but he couldn't find the words. He stared at the glass, as if waiting for the wine to speak to him, but the man-wine conversation would take place in silence. In that moment, Paolo discovered wine in a way he had never known it.

Of the hundreds of wines Paolo had enjoyed, many of them good, they were mostly peasant stock. His father sold their grapes to local wineries and the dell'Uco family received some wine in return with the payment. Paolo knew the local Tuscan wines were good – who could argue with the success of region's wines on the world market – but he did not often have access to the best of Tuscany. Here, in this bottle of Ceretto Barolo, he discovered what it was to enjoy the best wine a region had to offer.

The moment – and the wine's affect on Paolo – was not lost on Stefano, for whom this legendary "grape juice" was a passionate undertaking. He glanced at Paolo, mused silently about what he was thinking, and took a sip from his own glass. Just then Stefano smiled, realizing that this wine was the only thing so far that evening that had taken his nephew's attention off of Nicki.

Rita and Nicki were too interested in the food on their plates to bother with Paolo's thoughts or Stefano's ruminations. The women handed the platter of antipasti back and forth and drew their portions of Gasse that Rita had prepared.

When her immediate hunger pains were satisfied, Nicki turned to Paolo.

"So, you're Rita's nephew. How old are you?"

The question seemed a bit impetuous and left Paolo feeling a bit like a child, so he straightened up and spoke in a manly voice, saying he was twenty-three years old.

"Hmm," Nicki said, adding in a teasing tone. "The same as me," although Rita and Stefano knew she was just twenty.

Nicki was self-assured and confident in her handling of men; she apparently had much experience in fending them off. She matched her extraordinarily good looks with a keen intelligence. Not one that had been honed in the classrooms of the university but one that was enlightened by life's experiences. She was bright and quick at math, but even quicker at appraising men's attentions.

Turning to Rita, Nicki said in an offhand manner, "Francesco will be there next week."

"He's my boyfriend," Nicki explained to Paolo, tossing off a slight smile to convey the message to Paolo.

"He'll be where?" Paolo asked.

"In Alba," said Rita. "For the truffle season. Francesco's father is one of the best truffle hunters in Piedmont, and they all gather in Alba to sell their treasures and take part in the truffle festival."

Paolo was quickly lost but tried to catch on. He'd heard of truffles, but had never tasted any. Stefano turned into the "foodie" that he was and launched into a story about the legendary tuber, a subterranean growth that was so aromatic that a single shaving can make an entire dish come alive.

"The scent of truffles is so wonderful that, in an entire room, I can tell when even a single dish has used it."

Rita laughed doubtfully, wanting to spare her husband embarrassment, although secretly she had to admit that the fragrance of fresh truffles is so remarkable that even she can pick up the scent from far away.

Together, they educated Paolo with wondrous sighs and wild stories of the hunt – "Italians use dogs," Stefano noted sensibly, "not those obstreperous pigs of the French." Then Rita explained that they close the restaurant for three days in mid-week this time of year to go to Alba. Two trips are usually enough, she explained, so they would be closing the restaurant the first and second week of October, from Monday through Wednesday.

"Of course," Rita begins, "you will join us."

Nicki sat quietly, following the tales of the truffle festival with obvious interest. When Paolo asked if she is also going to Alba, she answered yes. Nicki was not with Ristorante Girasole in the previous year's truffle season, but she had her own personal reason to go this year.

"I'm looking forward to some time with Francesco," she said, then sipped again from the glass of Barolo.

22

PIAZZA RISORGIMENTO

*A*fter sleeping through most of his days since coming to Alba, he welcomed the evenings more than ever. Most Italian towns come alive after sunset, the lights of the cafés twinkling back at you from side streets, the sounds of music mingling from opposing corners of the piazze, the clink of plates and glasses at sidewalk tables, and the lively chatter of the people walking by.

Life was something like this back in his country, but stiffer and less friendly. The Italians had a way of making life sparkle. They took misfortune in stride – ever since the heyday of the Roman Empire, they've had their share of misfortune – and they reveled in good fortune. But through it all they laughed, loved, and played, as if enjoying each day was itself a victory.

He relaxed at a table in the Piazza Risorgimento with a satisfied smile and thought about the truffles that he – they – had secreted in the warehouse outside this humble city. And he wondered whether the Albese knew yet what had happened to them. He had heard some vague comments on the street, but couldn't make it out in Italian. It sounded like they were talking about truffles; in any case, it was always the men, always dressed in rough clothes, and always with the sound of concern in their voices.

But he also wondered how her end of the plan was going. She said her part was done early, getting the program, and she was just helping him with the harvest because they needed to move quickly.

The man had to admit he needed help because she wanted so many of the damn truffles.

"Why do we need so many?" he asked her once.

"They're part of the plan," was all she'd say. He knew the plan, and could piece together a strategy as well as she could, but she insisted that they collect more truffles than seemed necessary.

It was as if she wanted to damage the annual crop, whether they needed to or not.

That's the part that didn't seem to agree with the plan: "We were in it for the money, right?" he thought.

23

LAST NIGHT IN GENOA

Rita, Stefano, Paolo, and Nicki worked hard at Ristorante Girasole, as Paolo picked up lessons in the front and back of the restaurant. His experience with consumables was at the raw end of production, growing and picking grapes, and it didn't matter what he thought of the buyers and the end while he was still back at the farm. But people who spend hard-earned money to eat a fine meal expect to be treated to good food and friendly service.

Paolo spent most of his time in the kitchen with Stefano, while Rita worked both in the kitchen and in the dining room. Nicki served tables and only appeared in the kitchen to place or pick up an order. Stefano managed the wine inventory and drew the bottles from the racks, but Nicki delivered them to the guests, cutting the capsule and drawing the cork with practiced expertise.

At times, Paolo was drawn to the front to help serve a large order but otherwise spent his orientation to restaurant work in the back. It was hard work, not the physical labor he was accustomed to at his father's side, but he spent many hours on his feet and he had to be more careful with the plates, platters, and trays than the rough-hewn farm implements he used at home. He was not always successful.

The dining room cleared a bit earlier on Sunday than previous days, and the foursome went through the usual routine cleaning up and clearing the restaurant for the next business day. In this case, the doors wouldn't open again until Thursday while Rita, Stefano, Nicki and Paolo traveled to Alba, but Rita's knack for order demanded that everything in the front and back of the restaurant be presentable and ready for its first guests four days later.

At each dinner they shared after closing, Stefano produced a new bottle of wine. Paolo was years away from gaining his mentor's level of understanding of the vinous treasure, but he was eager to use these companion dinners to explore the subject and learn more from Stefano – and from tasting the wines.

"Tasting wine is like learning to play the piano," Stefano said, adding with a chuckle, "you have to practice." And with that he lifted the glass to his lips and continued - - "to practice."

On that particular Sunday night, while they enjoyed salted anchovies and Ciuppin, a traditional Ligurian fish soup, Stefano thought it best to share bottle of Pigato. This yellowish-gray-green wine was simple and straightforward, but it leaned toward a slightly salty flavor which complimented the anchovies.

For years, Paolo had followed his father's "first rule of wine-food pairing" – drink what you like – and his father used this rule to justify having a peasant red wine with every meal. There was nothing wrong with the rule, better to drink what you want than have a wine you don't like just because someone else thinks it's right for the dish.

But this approach to serving wine may also withhold much of the potential pleasure of the meal. Paolo recalled recent meals at home and admitted that he liked the wine and loved his mother's cooking, but now that he was experiencing Rita's fine food matched with Stefano's choice of wines, he realized another rule of wine.

In deference to Dito – someone Stefano respected for his age, hard work, and wisdom – Stefano was willing to call it the "second rule of wine-food pairing" – drink the region.

"Grapes are grown in the same soil and climate as the fruit and vegetables of the region, and in the same soil and climate as the grass that the animals graze on," Stefano explained. "And," he added with a finger pointed to the heavens, "the same soil from which the great chefs of the region are grown. The wines from each region are made to match the food prepared in that region.

"Over the centuries of cooking and eating, Italians have evolved an understanding of what flavors match well, and in each region the cuisine and winemaking practices evolve alongside one another."

When Nicki pointed out that "drink the region" also applied to France, Greece, and other wine producing countries, Stefano only shrugged. At that moment, Paolo saw his father's own gestures come out in his countryman.

"Of course, but we have evolved farther," Stefano replied with unapologetic national pride.

Rita was more generous to her fellow Europeans, and added a rejoinder, "Italian food relies more on fresh ingredients than the French. Where they focus on sauces, we focus on direct connection to the soil, bringing our vegetables and meats to the table in simpler form, preserving their natural beauty and flavor."

"So the flavors of the soil are there," Stefano said, "and so the wine matches the food more directly."

More conversation followed, some comparing the countries that compete on the world market for the greatest wines, with a proud nod to the wines of the Italian peninsula. "It's not called Enotria for nothing," Stefano concluded, referring to Italy's ancient name, which translates to "land of wine."

They cleaned up the table, washed the dishes and, under Rita's watchful eye, put everything away in its proper place. She circled the kitchen one more time, surveying the stacks of plates and pots, and approved. Then they retired for the night.

Retiring as restaurateurs usually did – late – it was a short night.

24

THE HEART OF LE LANGHE

The next morning they met early at Genoa Piazza Principe and boarded the train for Alba. It was a local train and would make more stops than the *rapido* that connected larger cities, but the company was genial and they had lots of stories to keep them company.

Stefano regaled the group with fabulous stories of the wine and truffles from Piedmont, specifically *le Langhe*, the Langhe hills known for these treasures. He talked spiritedly about the muscular Barolo and elegant Barbaresco wines, adding much detail that showed his appreciation for the lesser-known red wines made from the same grape, nebbiolo.

"It's named after the fog," he said, *la nebbia*, "because without the cooling effect of the morning fog this magical grape might not reach the pinnacle of wine." Stefano admitted to his love of other Italian wines, but "nothing, nothing at all, can compare to those from Piedmont."

And he swooned when discussing the hidden wealth of truffles in the soil of *le Langhe*. Rita was accustomed to her husband's passionate attachment to the tuber, and shared his love of cooking with truffles, but Stefano's enthusiasm and eagerness to join the truffle hunt was unparalleled.

As the wheels of the train clicked down the track and the foursome considered his stories, Stefano added, "It's like sampling a savory bit of heaven."

Paolo doubted the true worth of these "mushrooms" as he called them, but Stefano just said, "You wait."

They arrived at the train station in Piazza Trento e Trieste outside of Alba just after noon and emerged from the train among the crowds of people drawn to Alba every year during the truffle harvest.

Rita and Stefano had regular accommodations at Locanda Cortiletto d'Alba, on the Corso Michele Coppino in the heart of the city, and arranged for two more rooms for Paolo and Nicki. Cortiletto's floor plan was simple but inviting in a very Italian design. The office was small, recognizing the little importance attached to that function in Italian hotels. But its size left room for more important accoutrements, like the enclosed terrazzo and below-ground cantina that served as both its wine cellar and restaurant.

Rita and Stefano climbed the stairs to their room while Paolo and Nicki rose one more flight to their separate rooms on the next floor. Paolo enjoyed the closeness of this possibility, but Nicki was curt about shutting her door, curt enough to make a clear point to her male traveling companion.

They had agreed to tarry only a few minutes, then meet again on the terrazzo to explore Alba. Rita and Stefano knew it well; Nicki had some familiarity with the town afforded by visiting Francesco. Paolo was new to the town and was anxious to begin a tour of the streets.

They exited the Cortiletto and took an immediate right turn onto Via Gastaldi, a side street that led them to the center of Alba. Paired off on the sidewalk, Paolo had another opportunity to get to know Nicki, and began to appreciate her wit and stories of life in Genoa. They angled through the streets based on Rita and Stefano's knowledge of the town and wound up in the Piazza Risorgimento, the center of town that sported several restaurants, the office of tourism, and a grand church that dominated the piazza with its façade and bell tower.

Passing through the piazza and taking a right turn at the northern corner of the square, Stefano made a sudden stop and spun on his heel toward a door. Pulling it open just as Paolo recognized that it was a restaurant, Stefano called out to a man just inside, and they shared a warm embrace. Fabrizio, a stocky man with the girth of a successful chef, was obviously the owner of Antico Caffè Calissano. He immediately turned his attention to Rita who received a gentler hug and a kiss on both cheeks.

Looking directly at Stefano, Fabrizio said, "Don't ever come here without her," pointing to Rita. "I'll treat you nice and serve you the best food in Piemonte, but not without bella Rita!"

Rita smiled and another hug followed, then Fabrizio looked over her shoulder and saw Nicki standing in the doorway. Rita's back was to Nicki, but she could tell by the look on the owner's face what he was seeing. Rita pushed him away and, with a playful slap on the shoulder, said, "You unfaithful pig!" then laughed at her joke while Fabrizio blushed.

Stefano introduced Nicki and Paolo, pointed out that Paolo was Rita's *nipote*, and Fabrizio immediately launched into an exaggerated welcome for Nicki's benefit. She smiled, familiar with the attention, but deferred to Rita and Stefano.

"I'll feed you the best truffle dish you've ever had," he promised, never pausing to doubt his own superlatives.

"Truffles," Stefano asked with amused uncertainty. "This early in the day?"

Clapping him on the shoulder, Fabrizio told the others, "He'll eat truffles for breakfast too, if I opened Antico Caffè that early, and probably with his Ratafià at night!" exclaimed Fabrizio, referring to a fruity distilled liqueur enjoyed by Piemontese as a nightcap.

Rita stood quietly smiling while the men played out their game, then told Fabrizio that they would return later that night, for the best dinner he could serve! Fabrizio smiled, accepting her acknowledgment and picking up her subtle challenge.

"Si, *stanotte*," he said, "tonight!"

They emerged from Antico Caffè Calissano to join the crowds gathering in the late afternoon. They caught hints of German and Japanese among the boisterous Italian voices, and they saw children running through the square with parents in quick pursuit. Banners were strung across several of the side streets announcing the upcoming Truffle Festival, and they saw various shops that specialized in culinary goods had begun to shift their products to truffles.

Rita couldn't resist the magnetism of the *tartufo*. She stopped occasionally and peered at the products in the windows and came away with a disappointed look.

"They're small, and there aren't many of them," she said.

"Well, it's early in the season, so the *tartufi* would be smaller, but I don't think the shopkeepers would be holding out on us," Stefano said, with a light chuckle.

As they walked along, they picked up bits of conversation that often centered on truffles. There were more than a few comments about the crop, how small it was, and how unusual that was. Rita and Stefano knew they wouldn't be able to talk to the *trifolài* until the next morning, so they would have to wait to get more definitive information on these rumors.

25

PAOLO'S FIRST TIME

That evening they returned as promised to Antico Caffè Calissano. Fabrizio was busily breezing through his dining room, ostentatiously waving his arms and beaming his smile across the room, acting more like a visiting celebrity than a chef.

Stefano looked at his wife, and smiled reassuringly. He knew she was better in the kitchen than Fabrizio, but she didn't make such a show of it in the dining room.

She saw his smile and, in response, said, "But you have to admit, he's good."

Fabrizio swept over to the door and seated his new guests in a favored spot by the window and then disappeared into the kitchen.

Soon afterward, a young man delivered a clay pot of *bagna cauda* – a sauce made of butter, olive oil, garlic and anchovies – and a platter of cut raw vegetables and rustic bread for dipping. An unlabeled carafe of white wine accompanied this first course and the diners were quieted by the largesse. Soon, Carne all'Albese – thinly sliced veal with drizzles of lemon juice and olive oil – arrived and was served around the table, devoured along with another bottle of white wine.

By now, with the appetite initially sated and the wine serving to relax them, the conversation began again.

"Fabrizio probably does make the best food in all of Piemonte," said Rita, "but I will never admit it to him."

"Why not?" asked Nicki. "If he's that good."

"You see how big his head is already!" Rita remarked with a smile and a wave in the direction of the kitchen. "If he only knew that the best chef in Genoa thought he was the best chef in Alba …" and she let her voice trail off with the self-congratulatory quip.

With a bite of food in his mouth and the wine glass in his hand, Stefano grinned at his wife. She was still so beautiful and so lively. He wondered at times how he could have landed such a perfect partner.

Their stomachs slowly filling up, the foursome began to relax just as a large platter of pappardelle arrived. Paolo's eyes grew wide as saucers before the waiter was even halfway to the table.

"It's Pappardelle Tartufo," said Stefano, with the look of a child on Christmas morning. "Pasta is not as common in the north as it is elsewhere in Italy, but tossed in butter and only a touch of salt, it is the best way to enjoy the savory brilliance of truffles."

"Is that all they can talk about, truffles?" He was sitting at a table just ten feet from these self-important foodies and heard every word. He had to admit truffles are good, but – well, who was he kidding. He'd never had real truffles before.

"Perhaps on this trip," he muttered to himself. *"I can afford it."* The thought brought a smile to his face.

"Oh, yes," he whispered, *"Soon I will be able to afford it."*

It was the aroma of these exotic treasures that had caught Paolo's attention and turned his eyes in the direction of the approaching waiter. It was true, he thought, you could smell them from across the room! As with his first scent of Ceretto Barolo, Paolo's attention was drawn away from Nicki and focused on the food on his plate. She had enjoyed the wonders of truffles before, but was not the expert that Rita and Stefano were.

It is never easy matching a wine with truffles. The potent aromas called for a rich wine, but the subtle affect the truffles had on the dish called for a more balanced, possibly lighter wine. Stefano was all too familiar with this duality of flavors, and he smiled in Paolo's direction and knew that Dito's "first rule of wine-food pairing" was appropriate here.

A big Barolo or even an elegant Barbaresco would have overpowered the essence of this dish, so Stefano asked instead for a bottle of Altare Barbera d'Alba, another Piedmontese classic red wine but lighter in body.

The meal lasted nearly two hours and Rita, Stefano, Nicki, and Paolo were ready to retire to their hotel for a light siesta. A gulp of espresso assured that they would make it back to Cortiletto d'Alba without falling asleep, and they bid goodbye to Fabrizio.

"I'll see you *domani,* tomorrow, when we are competing for truffles in the piazza," he said, and he shook hands and shared hugs all around.

They walked back to the hotel a bit more slowly than they had walked in anticipation of the midday meal. At this point, they were full of food and pleasantly appeased with wine. Rita and Stefano held hands and walked close to each other.

Cortiletto d'Alba was quiet at this hour; its American guests were still exploring the nightlife of the town while its Italian guests had decided to turn in for the evening. Stefano buzzed the foursome into the locked terrazzo and all bade sweet dreams for a long-awaited night's sleep.

26

A CIVILIZED HUNT

All four of the visitors from Genoa had no trouble falling quickly to sleep that night. They were still tired from their own work at Ristorante Girasole and counted on this first night in Alba to catch up.

The next morning, Rita and Stefano awoke relaxed and rejuvenated. They were here on a mission, and it was one of their favorite missions on the calendar. Here, that day, they would "harvest" their own truffles and set up a fall menu that the people of Genoa would cheer for months to come.

Nicki awoke restless. She had not yet connected with Francesco, her real reason for the trip to Alba. She showered and slipped into comfortable clothes and even more comfortable shoes, knowing that the day would mean much walking and standing.

Paolo slept fitfully and was as energized as his aunt and uncle. He had never been to Alba, nor even the region of Piedmont, and he was discovering wines and food he had only heard about before. He paced the room for a few minutes, counted his new discoveries and compared this life to what he had at home. His cell phone rang in his pocket.

"*Pronto,*" he said lifting the small flip phone to his ear.

"Paolo," came his mother's voice. "*Come stai?*" she asked, how are you?

"*Bene, bene.*"

"Are you eating well? Have you arrived in Alba yet?"

"Mama, the food is wonderful, and the wine, oh, this is the best wine I have ever tasted. Mama…" he continued, until Catrina cut him off.

"Si, si, Paolo. I know the food is good. Rita is one of the best chefs there is. But I want to hear about you."

"Mama, we're going to meet the truffle hunters this afternoon, and it's been a long trip, and I need to get some sleep."

Then he added, "Is papa there?"

"Si," his mother replied, knowing that Dito was still torn by Paolo's departure and didn't want to talk to him. "He's here but he's out in the shed," she lied.

But she didn't lie well enough. Paolo heard it in her voice. His father was probably sitting in the room with her, listening to only half of the conversation, and Paolo quickly replayed his mother's words hoping that they were phrased in a way that would comfort his father.

They ended the conversation soon after, and Paolo sat on the edge of the bed. Paolo's eyes closed and he dozed off again, but was interrupted by a light tapping on his door.

In his half-awake state, it seemed to come to him from the end of a long tunnel. Paolo was temporarily disoriented. The room wasn't his, nor was it the room he occupied at Zia Rita's house. Shaking his head, he heard Stefano's voice, followed by a softer, feminine voice that he recognized from his dream.

Rising quickly and answering the door, Paolo peered out at his two visitors. Stefano had his hands on his hips and Nicki held her hand up to her mouth to hide her grin. Paolo twisted sideways to sneak a quick look in the mirror and soon understood her mirth. He was disheveled, his hair stood on end, and his eyes still had sleep in them.

Stefano and Nicki were dressed and ready for the afternoon in the piazza, and he looked like a character from a sleep study.

"Get dressed," Stefano commanded, though his tone was more forgiving. "We'll meet you in Piazza Savona in ten minutes." Nicki just smiled and gave Paolo a loving pat on the arm as she turned to go.

As ordered, Paolo made it to Piazza Savona in ten minutes. It was only a few blocks from the hotel but in a different direction from their trek earlier, so Paolo had to ask directions to find it.

Truffle hunters work in secrecy, preferring to hunt during the night and early morning hours to hide their hunting grounds from others. But Rita and Stefano hunted for their truffles in the market square, in Piazza Savona, on Via Maestra, and other avenues known to truffle hunters and buyers alike. Here, on their first afternoon in Alba, the bounty from the night before was being offered for sale.

Piazza Savona was a long-used, little-kept secret place for truffle hunters to sell their crop. Half of the truffle harvest was sold through legal channels – these sellers possess a *tesserino* or license – but another half of it was conveyed hand to hand, from hunter to buyer, along these streets. In the Piazza Savona, sellers strode the square with eyes dancing across the crowd, eager to spot someone who appeared to be looking for a truffle or two. Some hand signals were known, and certain truffle hunters were easily recognized, but the unmistakable clue was a man with a large coat and bulging pockets - - pockets filled with the elegant provisions.

Rita and Stefano approached a hunter, known as *trifolào,* and opened the discussion. Paolo was introduced, as was Nicki, but Rita and Stefano were more interested in their catch than in exchanging pleasantries. From the edges of the conversation Paolo and Nicki could detect signs that the sale was not going well. They leaned in a bit to catch more detail, and just then Nicki jumped.

Paolo spun around to see a tall young man with long black wavy hair standing behind them, a large grin on his face and his hands on the small of Nicki's back. This must be the thus-far absent Francesco.

Nicki jumped into Francesco's arms, shared a warm and longing kiss, then separated reluctantly to introduce Paolo. The men shook hands while Rita and Stefano distracted their gaze from the truffle transaction to see what the commotion was. Stefano, playing the role of protective father for the group, excused himself from the sale and stepped aside to be introduced.

"This is Francesco," Nicki said, with an unmasked tinge of pride in her voice.

"*Mi piacere*," Stefano said, nice to meet you.

Nicki had called Francesco from the hotel and said to meet them at the piazza that afternoon. He joined them to be with Nicki, but also to serve as agent for his father's own truffle harvest. His father, Tomaso, was a farmer whose fruit and vegetables supplied many of the restaurants in Alba, but he learned the truffle business from his father – and he had inherited his father's secret truffle grounds.

While truffle hunters' secrecy is legendary, they are also supremely superstitious. Finding gastronomic treasures buried in the dirt calls for both human notions. They work at night to cloak their actions and to hide the specific location of their truffle fields, and they offer prayers that seem to blend Catholic dogma with pagan ritual to ensure a good harvest.

And none of this could be done without the aid a strong olfactory sense, stronger than the one possessed by humans. Smelling the shavings of a fresh truffle across a restaurant dining room may be a simple feat for humans, but ferreting out the same tubers while they are still under the ground requires a being that is super-human.

A pig.

Well, the truffle hunters used to employ pigs, whose snouts were so effective that they could find even small truffles at the base of the favored trees, the most common breeding ground for these little chef's delights. But pigs are big and heavy enough to get the better of a simple farmer, and many truffles disappeared into the mouths of the pigs before the hunter could wrestle the animal away from the find.

So in recent years, *trifolài* employed well-trained dogs whose manners were more civilized than the pigs and whose strength could be bested by the humans on the other end of the rope.

But here, in the Piazza, it didn't matter whether the hunter used a dog or a pig, Rita and Stefano – as hunters in their own right – just wanted to score some truffles for their restaurant.

27

PIAZZA SAVONA, ALBA

Paolo was absorbing information about truffles and their history in a rush, another distinct difference from his unhurried work in a vineyard that never seemed to change. *Trifolài* were the kings of gastronomy, even though their treasures would ultimately be transformed by the chefs who delivered these white diamonds to the table.

Past the introductions, Stefano was more interested in the conversation that Rita was having with the hunter, a discussion that had become quite spirited. It seems the hunter wanted an astronomical sum for this year's truffles, a price that was nearly triple the past year.

"*Non ci sono tartufi!*" he exclaimed, "there are no truffles," throwing his hands up before shrugging his shoulders, admitting that there must be some, or else he would have nothing to sell.

The thief was walking through the piazza and overheard this. His Italian was a bit rusty, but he knew what was being said. He almost smirked, but knew that would be a dangerous "tell," like the Americans say about a gambler's tick that would give him away. So he walked on.

Rita immediately suspected that he was trying to gouge them and demanded to see a sample. The man reached into his pocket, in a coat that sagged under the weight of bulky truffles gathered in every compartment, and withdrew a lump that resembled a gnarled potato. It had a rough, wrinkled surface and was still dusty from the earth. Rita brought it to her nose and her eyebrows lifted. It was clearly an excellent example, aromatic and fresh from the morning's hunt, but she again questioned the reason for the price.

"There are so few truffles this year, and we've been out many times," the hunter explained. "We don't know what's happened, but there are far fewer than in other years."

His protests were generating some sympathy from Rita. Not enough to convince her to pay the high price, though.

"Is there a fungus?" she asked, then immediately regretted it, because the *tartufi bianchi*, the prized white truffle from this part of Italy, truly is a fungus. But her meaning wasn't lost on the hunter.

"No, signora, there's nothing wrong in the ground. The earth smells the same. But," he said with a downward glance, "there are no truffles." He acted as though he had not only lost his harvest but a dear friend.

A short man with long black hair flopping down on his forehead approached from the fringe of the discussion. Francesco recognized Alfonso and introduced him to everyone in the group. He was a fruit dealer and, like Tomaso, he supplied produce to the restaurants and grocers in the area. Alfonso greeted each with a smile and joined the exchange between Rita, Stefano, and the truffle hunter.

"Si, it's terrible," said Alfonso. "Just as the truffles were coming in, the supply seemed to vanish. No one knows what has happened and, in my own business, I am suffering because I would have represented the *trifolài* in this year's market."

Tomaso appeared from around the corner and joined his son Francesco, just as Alfonso excused himself and walked away. Tomaso greeted Nicki with a warm embrace and was introduced to Paolo, but he was reluctant to talk to Rita and Stefano while they were still engaged with the truffle hunter in conversation. The people of Alba knew one another and the farmers were often friends, but they hunted for truffles alone and when these gastronomic gems were the subject of conversation, they kept apart.

"I overheard the talk. Si," Tomaso intoned, then switched to English, "the truffle harvest is tiny this year, a mere trifle of years past."

Despite her concerns about the harvest, Tomaso's comment brought a smile to Rita's lips, knowing that Tomaso's sometimes halting English disguised an expert understanding of the subtleties of the language. She knew that "trifle" was derived from "truffle" and was a code used by early hunters to hide the importance of their find. The inauspicious outward appearance of a truffle, with its dusty, knobby look, carried the theme that it was nothing, and the holder would guardedly explain to suspicious people "it's just a trifle."

"Si," Francesco joined in, "it's like someone just stole the *tartufi* right out of the ground."

Stefano turned to Tomaso. "Do you believe there's nothing that can be done? The harvest is truly down and we have to pay these prices?"

Tomaso shrugged his shoulders, a time-honored gesture among Italians that conveyed many things. First, that the respondent is unsure how to answer the question. Second, to indicate a certain divine influence, so what's the point of answering. Lastly, to use a theatrical move to stall for time to find the right words.

"I have to charge more, too," Tomaso finally offered. "If I only have one-third the crop, but my landlord still wants three-thirds of the mortgage payment..." He let the sentence die without voicing the obvious conclusion.

28

DINNER AT LA PIOLA

Rita and Stefano broke away from the others to find more *trifolài* to talk to. Walking slowly toward the outer edges of Piazza Savona, they whispered back and forth, trying to analyze the problem and yet find a solution to theirs: Ristorante Girasole was renowned for its truffle menu in October. Unless these two could hunt down more truffles, the year's menu would be embarrassing.

Tomaso and Paolo stood longer talking about the harvest as Paolo soaked in mountains of stories and anecdotes about the wondrous tuber. Tomaso explained the science of truffle organisms, called mycology, and explained to Paolo the less scientific knowledge that had become part of tradition and folklore among the Albese and, more importantly, among the *trifolài*. Paolo listened intently, impressed by the detail that this man, a farmer like his father, knew about the subterranean prize that he brought to market each year. And Paolo thought about his own father.

"Mio papa," he said, "grows grapes. We don't make our own wine, but our vineyard is one of the best in Tuscany." The pride in his voice took even Paolo by surprise. He smiled to himself at the realization that, only a few days ago, he wanted to divorce himself from those vines forever.

"Bravo," was Tomaso reaction, and smile spread across his lips as he clapped Paolo on the shoulder. "Tuscan wine is *fantastico!*"

They continued their conversation about truffles, but Nicki and Francesco decided that such work was not foremost on the minds, and they departed the piazza for some personal time.

"You must learn the difference between the French truffles and the Italian truffles," said Tomaso. "I'm not saying the French have nothing to be proud of, but – truly – the Albese white truffle is as a diamond, the French Périgord a garnet."

Tomaso patiently explained to Paolo about the difference between the black Périgord truffles of France and the white truffles found there in northern Italy. The *Tuber melanosporum* – France's black truffle – might be "very nice, it might work with some dishes," he admitted, though his compliment was clearly only a consolation prize.

"But the *Tuber magnatum* here is the king of all truffles." Tomaso continued his praise from what was obviously a much-recited lecture on the majestic properties of the fungus, occasionally referring back to the French black truffle if only to make his point. Paolo listened carefully, his attention driven in part by his recent and still vivid encounter with his first truffle dish – not insignificantly with the Italian white truffle.

"But I've heard people here arguing about whether the truffle should be cooked or served fresh. What is the right way?"

Tomaso waved his hand dismissively. "Ask Fabrizio a question like that. He's the chef, I'm the hunter. Besides, Italians argue about everything."

After a time, Tomaso decided he needed to return to his work – selling the small collection of truffles he had with him – and he left Paolo to ponder this new world he had entered. Paolo wandered away from Rita and Stefano, wandered about the piazza, watching the people interact, peering into shop windows, and reading the menus of the restaurants that lined the edges of the square. Then he decided to explore the neighborhoods of Alba.

Nicki and Francesco had already gone their way, and Rita and Stefano were still in Piazza Savona searching for a decent cache of truffles for their restaurant.

The early evening came upon them, as each of them, singly or in pairs, wanderedoff in pursuit of different discoveries. But around eight o'clock, Rita and Stefano, Paolo, Nicki and Francesco met at La Piola for dinner. By prior arrangement, Tomaso joined them at this establishment on the Piazza Risorgimento, a restaurant that reminded Rita and Stefano somewhat of their own. A restaurant that combined traditional dishes with more modern surroundings, and one whose dining room was usually filled by tourists and locals alike.

Rita and Stefano were anxious to talk to Tomaso about their conversations with other *trifolài*, and Paolo wanted to ask about Alba and relate what he had seen from his travels around the city. Nicki and Francesco were quiet, but sat affectionately close and seemed privately happy.

Tomaso ordered a bottle of Ceretto Moscato d'Asti Vignaioli di San Stefano, a local sparkling wine, to begin the feast. Packed with fruit on a lightly dry frame, this wine was perfect for food but doubled as an aperitif, which suited this table of hungry patrons very well.

Rita began.

"Tomaso, is it true that the entire crop is smaller this year? Could it be a plague, or infestation in certain areas?"

Tomaso looked down at the table while gently twirling the liquid in his wine glass. He thought for a moment and then looked up at Rita.

"We hope that is the case. Of course we don't want an infection to sweep through the *tartufaie*" – the groves of oak and hazelnut trees around whose roots the best and most prolific truffle catches could be found.

Slowly, Tomaso shook his head side to side. "Not like the Great Plague." He didn't have to say anything more. Rita and Stefano understood the reference well enough. The Great Plague referred to the infestation of phylloxera, the root louse carried to Europe in the 19th century on American grapevines, a pest that wiped out centuries-old vineyards, devastating the culture of wine for decades and nearly ending Europe's thousand-year reign as the world's finest wine producing continent.

Francesco and Paolo also understood the reference, since both of them hailed from agricultural families, but the subtle reference was lost on Nicki.

"The Great Plague was something that nearly destroyed the vineyards," he began, shaking his head side to side. His youth did not diminish the passion of his report.

"The vines were dying, emaciated, in pain. We tried everything. We used sulphur. We flooded the vineyards to drown the pest," he continued with his prayerful recounting, as if he was actually there during the late-19th century disaster.

"Then we realized that the American vines back in the United States were not suffering. We realized that the only way to save our vineyards was to transplant our own vines onto the American rootstock that had brought this pest to our land."

Everyone at the table looked at the pained expression on Paolo's face, but it was Tomaso who decided to return the conversation to the problem at hand, their own "great plague."

"We hope there is no plague, and so we search together sometimes, breaking a tradition of secrecy that goes back many generations, so that we can find the truth. If some *tartufaie* are still producing, and some are not, that would mean the worst.

"But it is not so." Tomaso allowed a tense smile, shrugged his shoulders in the eternal Italian gesture meaning so many things. "We find no truffles, so either the *Il Peste* – the plague – is real or something else has gotten all our diamonds."

Food began to arrive at the table and their attention shifted to that. A platter called *selezione di salumi* arrived first, a broad array of sliced meat and cheese.

Rita ordered Tajarin con Burro, a delicate noodle served with melted butter. Before the waiter could get away, Stefano whispered something in his ear and, when the dish arrived, everyone at the table could smell the aroma of truffles on her pasta. The aroma didn't escape her attention but when she playfully poked Stefano, Paolo was surprised by the reaction. Stefano turned toward him and remarked that the *trifolài* have long considered truffles to be an aphrodisiac. Rita, catching his words to Paolo, blushed but didn't delay in helping herself to the dish.

The choice of menu items around the table focused on traditional Albese dishes, with venison and rabbit featured among them. Sauces were light and infrequent, as Italian chefs prefer to use herbs to bring out the flavors of the food.

Appropriately, the next bottle to arrive was Vietti Roero Arneis, a crisp, lively white wine that was perfectly suited to light- to medium-styled dishes. They ate and drank, traded stories about Alba in general and truffles in particular. But their discussion seldom wandered far from food and wine. Paolo listened more than he talked, and he drank in not only the fine wines of Piedmont but the traditions and culinary secrets of the region.

29

STORIES OF GLORIES PAST

After three hours spent around the table, the diners rose to leave. Rita and Stefano headed in the direction of Dario's, their favorite gelato shop, knowing that the short walk across the piazza and down the side street would be just enough exercise to make room for dessert.

Nicki slipped her hand through Francesco's arm, turned slightly to leave a gentle kiss on Paolo's cheek, and the pair wandered off for the evening *passeggiata*, a postprandial stroll that most Italians feel is as important as the meal itself.

Tomaso stood on the corner smoking a cigarette, blowing cool columns of blue smoke while providing closing comments to Paolo on the magic of the *tartufo*.

"Most people know there are four flavors: sweet, sour, salty, bitter. The best chefs are trained to combine these impressions to achieve the great flavors of the dish. But what is the mushroom? It's neither sweet nor sour, and certainly not salty or bitter."

He looked at Paolo as if he was waiting for an answer, but by then Paolo knew Tomaso's teaching method. He didn't expect the student to provide an answer, but he paused to let the question sink in.

With raised eyebrows Tomaso added, "And if the lowly mushroom can't be classed in this way, what can be said of the majestic *tartufo?*"

Tomaso cast his eyes down at the pavement, spat out a tiny thread of tobacco leaf that had escaped his cigarette, and brushed his lips with his hand. Still considering the question with his head down, he continued.

"The Asian chefs answered this question centuries ago, but we didn't listen."

Paolo didn't know where this proud Italian was going, but stayed rapt in the description.

"They call it umami, we call it savory. A word that describes flavors to remind us of fish oil, fermented seaweed, mushrooms...and truffles. The most interesting thing about savory accents is that too much overpowers the dish. Some people think that restricting risotto, for example, to only a few shavings of fresh truffle is *tirchio,* cheap. But more than that would ruin the flavor."

Paolo smiled slyly at Tomaso's knowledge of cuisine. "I thought you said to ask Fabrizio questions about cooking."

Tomaso smiled back, and he raised his shoulders in a single gesture to mean, "What do you think? I wouldn't learn?"

With that, Tomaso waved his cigaretted hand and bade Paolo "*buono sera,*" then wandered off into the night. Paolo was left to consider all that he had learned, and how he was going to apply this new knowledge to his life in Sinalunga.

The thought startled him. Paolo left his home to discover the world, but he already found himself absent-mindedly applying his new lessons to his return.

He began to walk alone, not the *passeggiata* that Italians preferred, in linked arms with loved ones, but the cool air of an autumn night in Alba was refreshing and he wasn't ready to return to his room at the Cortiletto d'Alba just yet.

It was in moments of solitude like this that Paolo thought of home. He didn't miss it, or at least that was not how he explained the thought, but he had new respect for what his father and mother did in Sinalunga. Paolo watched the people passing by, in couples or small families with children skipping to keep up with parents. He thought about his aunt and uncle who worked hard day and night, side by side, and about the hundreds of customers in Genoa who considered the Ristorante Girasole part of their everyday experience. And he thought about the self-assured Francesco who would yield the field to his father and – though taller than the older man – seemed to take a smaller position beside him.

Paolo found himself wondering about Nicki. He didn't remember anything said about her family, and he was deep in thought when a voice called out his name.

"Paolo!" It was coming from a dimly lit sidewalk café on a side street to his right. Peering down the via, he made out a waving hand, heard "*Vieni qui,*" "come here," and realized that it was Rita and Stefano relaxing at a café table.

Paolo walked past tables of lovers snuggling in the evening chill, a table of men in soccer jerseys who were celebrating the afternoon's victory, and an older couple whose comfortable closeness was evidence of many years of happy marriage. The *cameriere,* or waiter, was at their table when he reached his aunt and uncle, and Paolo reflexively ordered a Campari and soda, a common libation for Italians at any time of the day.

The drink arrived quickly, but tasted slightly different from the Campari and soda he was used to. Noticing his questioning look, Stefano chimed in, "It's called *la bicicletta*, the bicycle. In Piedmont it's customary to add a bit of white wine to this common Italian aperitif."

"Hmmm," Paolo said, but he liked the result.

From the stout aromas of Stefano's drink, Paolo could tell that he was drinking a Negroni, something that combines gin, vermouth, and Campari, and Rita was idling over what seemed a final glass of Prosecco, Italy's famed sparkling wine from the northeastern provinces.

"What did you do?" Rita asked, pairing her maternal instincts with friendly banter.

"*Non c'e nulla,*" he answered, "not much."

"Well," she continued, "I wish you would smile at that pretty girl at the next table," cocking her head in that direction. "Stefano thinks I haven't noticed his wandering eye."

Stefano protested but Rita dismissed it with a wave of the hand. Flirting is so common in Italy that men can't escape being caught in the act. And women can't deny drawing the flirtatious attention in the first place.

Paolo looked in the direction Rita indicated and smiled broadly. His aunt had good taste – and, it seems, his uncle did too – and the young man did as instructed. The pretty brunette let her eyes smile first, then allowed her lips to get into the response, then turned her attention back to the other girl at the table.

"*Il cameriere* seems very friendly with the other girl," Stefano told Paolo. "He's probably her boyfriend," suggesting that the brunette might be unaccompanied. After trying to help his nephew in courting ways, Stefano let his eyes wander in Rita's direction. It took only the ironic smile etched on Rita's lips for Stefano to realize that his awareness of the chemistry at the other table gave him away.

"Busted!" said Rita smiling, using the American slang word to show her husband what she knew all along.

Stefano let out a nervous laugh and stood to go inside and pay the bill. Left alone, Rita told Paolo that they were going back to the hotel, but that he didn't need to follow right away. Then she stood, took her scolded husband by the arm, and they walked away.

Watching them leave, Paolo turned his attention back to his drink. But when he raised the glass to his lips, his upturned eyes caught sight of the brunette smiling in his direction.

It didn't take long to get her name – Lucia – and Paolo bought a bottle of Albino Armani Moscato, a light, refreshing sparkling wine to share with her and her companion. They talked for an hour under the watchful eye of the *cameriere* before Paolo collected Lucia's phone number and address. Another hour and more conversation, and the girls decided it was time to go. Light hugs, a kiss on the cheek, and a wink had Paolo promising to call on her the next day, while he returned to Cortiletto d'Alba.

30

HUNTING FOR THE HUNTERS

With the activities of the day, an afternoon of snooping around among the *trifolài*, a long evening meal followed by drinks at the café, Paolo was still in a fog the next morning, so the banging at the door woke him from a deep sleep. He lifted himself up on his elbows, hazily recollecting where he was, and walked to the door. Pulling on the handle he expected to see Stefano – but Paolo was surprised to see the more diminutive Rita standing on the threshold.

"Did you forget?" she asked.

"Stefano and I are leaving today," Rita continued, "and we want to talk to Giorgio and Bruno before going to the train.

"Si, certo," he mumbled, *sure.* He knew they were leaving and remembered talking the night before about what he and Nicki would be tasked to do in their absence.

"Meet us outside Cortiletto as soon as you can." With that, Rita turned quickly and bolted down the stairs that led to her room.

When Paolo realized that he was being left in Alba with Nicki, he snapped out of the fog and raced to get showered and dressed.

Paolo swung through the hotel's breakfast room, swept a double espresso off the counter, and downed it in one gulp. By the time he reached the sidewalk, all four were present, including Francesco, whose presence reminded him that he would not be left completely alone with Nicki.

"It's important that you and Nicki keep trying to find some truffles," Rita said, looking back and forth at the two. Francesco was listening but not looking at Rita. "Just as well," she thought, "he had no ties to Ristorante Girasoldi."

"We'll talk to Bruno and Giorgio," Stefano chimed in, "and get some names of others you can talk to after we've left. It wouldn't hurt to talk to some storekeepers and chefs, to see what they've heard."

"Basically," Rita summed it up, "we want to you to meet the hunters and set up the sales – even start working on the prices – by the time we return."

They started off down Corso M. Coppino toward Via Gastaldi and Rita waved to a person up ahead.

"Giorgio is over there," she said, pointing at a middle-aged man with scruffy clothes, mildly unkempt hair, and a canvas hat pulled close upon his ears. They crossed the street to meet him, and were soon joined by Bruno, another hunter who was close friends with Giorgio. Bruno was slightly better dressed than Giorgio, but there was no mistaking that both of these men made their living from the earth.

"*Buon giorno. Come stai?*" asks Rita, "how are you?" "We bought truffles from you last year," she said, addressing both Giorgio and Bruno.

"And the year before that," added Bruno.

"What is the price this year?" Stefano asked. Both of the men regarded him with sheepish looks and seemed reluctant to reply.

Finally, Giorgio responded, quoting a price that was nearly three times last year's. Haggling began immediately, with Stefano acting suspicious and Rita responding like she had been stung by the price.

The *trifolài*, tried not to lose the deal altogether, explaining that they had mouths to feed and, with so few truffles this year, the price must go up.

"Scarcity names the price," said Bruno, lifting his shoulders to reinforce the point that he was not completely in control of the price of truffles this year.

"What happened?" Rita grilled. "Are we supposed to think that Alba, home to the greatest truffles in the world, has suddenly lost its crop?"

Giorgio looked at Bruno, a move that Stefano pounced on as an inept effort to conspire.

"Don't look at him for the answers," he stormed, and addressing Giorgio with a finger pointed at his chest, he asked, "How much did you bring in this year?"

Giorgio looked like a man caught on a witness stand, testifying against his brother.

"Maybe two kilos, looking down at his fingers, and last year it was 5.5 kilos."

Bruno leapt in to support his friend.

"And I have only three and a half kilos this year, only one-fourth of my crop from last year."

Stefano peppered them with questions: "Where did you look? Were the plots the same? What was the harvest like? And other queries that *trifolài* would not have had the temerity to ask one another. And with that, Giorgio and Bruno both responded with offense.

"Signore, we know our business," Bruno pushed back. "We are *trifolài*, the best in Alba," although his boast would be hard to corroborate. "We know where to look and what effect the weather will have. Don't ask us insulting questions. I tell you the crop is down!" he added with emphatic tones.

This retort gave Giorgio some time to compose himself, and his reply was more subdued.

"Stefano, we want to sell tartufi to you and Rita for your restaurant, and we would rather sell more than less, but they're not there."

The exchange went from hot to tepid, and all tempers cooled a bit. Paolo was a mere bystander, and Nicki knew enough to keep her place as hired help. Only Francesco stayed close to the debate, though he remained an observer.

The back-and-forth argument raged for about thirty minutes, some new information was shared, but Giorgio and Bruno had no option but to admit the truth: They had precious few truffles this year and had to make a living. When the conversation slowed a bit, Rita looked first at her husband, then at the ground. Stefano stared at the two hunters before him, as if he hoped that standing stubbornly there on the street would make the truffles magically appear.

Rita touched Stefano's arm and he looked at her. They exchanged some quiet words while Giorgio and Bruno stood waiting. Paolo watched all this with admiration. It seemed like a standard bartering session, one in which each party got some of what they were aiming for, and the result would be a slightly reduced price and a slightly smaller exchange of truffles. Which is why he was surprised at Rita's next statement.

"We can't buy them," she said, while Stefano looked on impassively. "We can't afford that. We don't buy solely for our own pleasure. We buy truffles for our restaurant. Basically, we buy truffles to resell them to our customers, and at this price, we would have to raise our menu prices so high that no one would come in."

Stefano wanted to put all this in perspective. "As hard as it is for us here, and you, all of us standing here in Alba to understand the crisis with truffles this year, our customers don't know – they wouldn't be able to understand – why the Ristorante Girasole was charging two or three times as much for the same dishes we have made our reputation on in the past."

By now, Francesco had receded from the immediate circle to become just a listener. Nicki brushed her shoe back and forth on the sidewalk, and Paolo stood transfixed. He was new to the magical powers of the truffle, and he was already witnessing the tuber at a crossroads. His early life and general background hadn't prepared Paolo to care so much about food, but in an epiphany that morning, he realized that he had already been drawn so far into the circle of Italy's grand cuisine that he was nervously wondering what this could mean for the next generation of food lovers.

Giorgio and Bruno made another feeble attempt to get the restaurateurs to reconsider. All four realized that Rita and Stefano weren't holding out simply for advantage; they were right – higher menu prices could doom the fall dining season.

Soon, the group disbanded. Muttering between themselves, Rita and Stefano tried to decide what they would do next. Francesco excused himself from the others, explaining that he had to help his father at the farm. And Paolo and Nicki fell in behind Rita and Stefano heading back to the hotel.

At the door of the Cortiletto d'Alba, Rita turned to Paolo to say that they were going upstairs to pack and would head to the train station to return to Ristorante

Girasole, and reminded him that he would remain in Alba with Nicki and try to sort out this mess with the truffles.

"We'll bring our cousin in to help in the restaurant this weekend. She knows her way around the kitchen," Rita said. "You two stay in Alba and see what you can find out about the truffles. Remember, we still need them; we're just not going to pay that kind of price."

31

ALBA AT NIGHT

That afternoon, following Rita and Stefano's departure for the train station at Piazza Trento e Trieste, Paolo and Nicki walked off to tour Alba and find out more about the missing truffles. There were many questions, but few answers. For their part, the *trifolài* were ambivalent. They didn't want to diminish the excitement about the truffle harvest, but they also couldn't deny the scarcity and the impact this had on the prices they must demand.

Most of the tourists who were now crowding Alba's streets knew very little about the problem and, if they did know, it seemed to matter little to them. Tourists were not the main market for the *trifolài*, who sold most of their crop to the restaurants, markets, and other Albese.

When it was time for dinner, Nicki and Paolo chose La Savona and settled in at a small table in the front corner by the window. They asked for a bottle of sparkling water, followed by a request for a bottle of Altare Barbera d'Alba.

The waiter delivered the wine bottle and pulled the cork, poured two glasses, but then put the bottle and both glasses on the sideboard next to their table. He departed, then returned with a bottle of sparkling water in his right hand, and two glasses grasped in his left. First he put the bottle down with a clunk at the edge of the table, then he quickly set the glasses down beside it. With a deft wrist action, he twisted off the cap from the bottle, and filled a water glass for each of them. In seconds, they were arranged next to Nicki and Paolo's settings, and the waiter spun around and left without a word.

Some truffle hunters came into the restaurant and sat at a table near the window. Their conversation was animated and occasionally punctuated by an Italian swear word, but since most Italians communicated with gusto, there was no reason to assume that this conversation was raking over the circumstances of the sudden disappearance of the truffles once more.

Nicki ordered dishes for both of them, and boldly veered off the printed list, knowing that a restaurant such as this was capable of making more than just what the menu recommended to uninitiated guests.

Cucina Borghese means local cooking, and anyone who knows their way around restaurants and Italian regional food knows how to find interesting dishes not offered to the tourists.

A small pot of *bagna caôda* arrived, surrounded by steamed vegetables. This was accompanied by a basket of rolls and oven-hot slices of *biova,* the large loaves of fresh bread common in this region. Paolo and Nicki both reached for bread to dip into the *bagna caôda.*

"So, what happens now?" Paolo asked.

"About what?" replied Nicki. She knew that he meant the matter of the truffles, but she combined the words with raised eyebrows and a flirtatious glance, just to get Paolo to blush. It worked. Nicki sometimes scolded herself for such acts of random flirting, but she justified it by reminding herself that practice makes perfect.

"I meant the truffle hunt," he stammered.

Just then, Alfonso walked past their table, stopped suddenly when he recognized Nicki and Paolo, and spun around to greet them.

"*Buona sera, signorina,*" he said reaching for Nicki's hand, as he offered Paolo only a nod. "And what brings the two of you to this restaurant."

Nicki didn't dislike Alfonso but thought of him as light and somewhat lacking in maturity. Francesco could have better friends, she thought, but then again, she didn't think it wise to interfere.

"We were hoping to hear some more rumors about the truffle problem, maybe even find someone who knows more than rumors," Paolo said, although he was seriously eyeing the menu as he spoke.

"Rita and Stefano had to return to Genoa, but they decided it would be a good idea for us to stay here, find out what we could, and help them resume their search for affordable truffles when they return next Monday."

A young woman sidled up to Alfonso and put her arm around his waist. She smiled sweetly and spoke in friendly terms. Alfonso wrapped his arm around her shoulders and introduced her as Lidia.

Lidia was pleasant and almost shy, finding herself the lone stranger in this group of friends. But Alfonso made it a point to include her in the conversation and Nicki warmed to her also. Her dark hair and hazel eyes set were a colorful contrast to her white complexion, and she seemed to have a genuine personality that made her easy to converse with. Alfonso was a bit flighty, Nicki thought. Perhaps this girlfriend would keep him grounded.

Alfonso and Lidia excused themselves, just in time for the main course to arrive.

Paolo and Nicki exchanged stories about their lives before the Ristorante Girasole and Alba. Paolo described the family farm, how his father labored in the vines every day, and how he wanted to go to America.

"Why America?" Nicki asked.

To Paolo, it seemed a strange question. "Doesn't everyone want to go to America?"

"I don't," she said, shrugging her shoulders to accentuate her lack of interest in such a plan. Nicki explained that everything she had ever wanted was in Italy. America was a nice place, she said – and she drew a jealous look from Paolo when she said she had already been to New York and Washington – but she couldn't live without the people, the culture, the family structure, the food, wine, and art of Italy.

"Would you leave all that behind?" she asked him.

Nicki might have wanted an answer from Paolo, but he needed more time to think, so he treated her question like it was rhetorical. And he thought about his family, his father, and how his mother seemed to loosen her bonds on him while somehow holding him tight to her breast.

Nicki told Paolo about her family's farm, the vegetables that they grew for themselves and for the *alimentarii*, the little grocery stores in the village, and how she and her brother and sister were proud of growing their own food.

"Being close to the earth was, by itself," she said, "a reward in life." Paolo noticed how she softened as she talked about that life before.

Then Nicki told Paolo about how her father had died working on the farm. She looked down at her plate, pushed the meat around a bit with her fork, and let out a little sigh.

She paused, and Paolo respected her with his silence. When she continued, Nicki explained how it had been an accident on the farm, something to do with the tractor and a malfunction.

She explained that she couldn't stay at the farm anymore. "I go home twice a year to see my mother, and I miss her so much." With this she couldn't fight back the tears that gathered on her eyelashes. She flicked her finger at one drop that threatened to spill onto her cheek.

They shared the rest of the dinner in greater silence, but still talked about their lives a bit. Paolo got to know more than the flirtatious charm he saw so often in Nicki.

32

MORNING PLANS

Morning seemed to come earlier than usual the next day. The excitement of the truffle festival created an indescribable energy that caught everyone up in it. The streets literally filled with tourists and hungry foodies, who were pouring into this quiet city every hour, many of whom did not want to miss the *Palio degli Asini*. The annual race featured donkeys commandeered by locals from the *borghi*, or neighborhoods, vying for the victory in a race that mixed humor, stubbornness, and pageantry.

The atmosphere was infectious and swept Paolo along. His thoughts were still on the truffle harvest and every so often his mind drifted back to the Rita's assignment. As the festival atmosphere mingled with his thoughts of missing truffles, he even wondered whether this tension added to the mood of the town during this season.

For her part, Nicki was less intrigued with the festival and focused more on the absence of Francesco. "He seems to be so distant," she thought, as she searched the crowd for signs of him.

Paolo and Nicki sized up the day and tried to decide who they could talk to after what little they got from Giorgio and Bruno, something to further the investigation and respond to some of Rita and Stefano's questions. Since the scheduled events of the truffle festival didn't begin until later in the day, Nicki tried to get Paolo back on track and refocused on the assignment they had regarding the mysterious disappearance of most of the truffle crop.

"We've got to find out more about the truffles," she said. "It's Saturday, the festival will occupy most of our attention – and the attention of the *trifolài* – and we need to find out more before they come back on Monday."

Paolo nodded in agreement, while Nicki's own attention was split looking for Francesco.

"Let's go to some of the restaurants," Paolo suggested. "Truffles mean more to them than anyone in this town. Surely they're already investigating the problem." It was an incontrovertible statement, and Nicki nodded assent.

A sonorous chirp from Nicki's cell phone called her attention and, looking at the display, she quickly punched in the "receive" button.

"Francesco, *tu dov'è? Perche? Lavori alla fattoría? Ancora? Quando ritornerai?*

Even though she cupped her hand over the phone – having a tiff with one's boyfriend is not what a girl wants others to hear – so she was muffling her words, but her tone alone convinced Paolo that she was angry.

She carried on a brief conversation, then softened a bit as Francesco's words seem to calm her. By the end of the call, Nicki smiled, nodded her head once again, and slowly put the phone back in her pocket.

"*Andiamo*," she said curtly, turning about and heading down the street without waiting to see if Paolo kept up. He did.

By now Paolo was accustomed to Nicki's blend of gentleness and command, so he shook his head with a chuckle, and caught up with her.

"Where are we going?" he asked.

"To Bottega del Caffè, in Via Alfieri." The name didn't mean anything to Paolo, but Nicki's purposeful stride made him choose simply to follow her and not ask any more questions.

After a brief two-block walk, they approached a sidewalk spread of umbrella-topped tables. Paolo took in the rich, lusty aroma of freshly brewed coffee before they came even with the wide-cast doors of Bottega del Caffè. Just as Nicki was turning in toward the interior of the café, she nearly walked into Lidia, who was talking over her shoulder and not watching where she was going.

"*Ciao, Nicki,*" Lidia said warmly. "How are you? We had the best meal last night. I told Alfonso we should follow you around to find the best places to eat."

Nicki laughed it off, but replied, "We just follow the suggestions of my employer, Paolo's aunt. She knows everything about food and, apparently, everyone in Alba who knows about food."

As Alfonso waved goodbye to the barista and joined Lidia at the door, they slipped sideways to allow Paolo and Nicki to enter, waving on their way out the door.

"Nicki spends a lot of time with him," Alfonso said, serving as protector for his friend Francesco.

"Well, maybe Francesco is not making himself available enough," countered Lidia.

Nicki walked up to the cashier and ordered a cappuccino and a double espresso for Paolo, by now knowing what her companion liked to drink in the morning.

Paying for the order, Nicki then took the ticket to the counter to present to the barista. With the deft motions of a man accustomed to filling hundreds of these orders each day, the barista swiftly produced a large steaming cup of cappuccino for Nicki, and a piping hot, though conspicuously smaller, cup of black liquid for Paolo.

They moved their treasure to a nearby table that was elevated for standing patrons, and Nicki looked around the room. Her eyes darted from table to table, then came to rest on a smallish man who wore a cap pulled down upon his head, and workman's clothes hung from his slight frame. Paolo shifted his gaze to the man but held his questions. In a moment, Nicki looked up at Paolo, cocked her head in the old man's direction, and walked over to greet him.

"Ciao, signore."

"Ciao, signorina," the man answered dubiously. There was a look of recognition in his eyes, but the strained look made it apparent that he couldn't place a name with the beautiful face gazing back at him. In seconds, Paolo appeared at the table also, merely following Nicki, but his appearance at the table produced a subtle alarm in the

old man. Now instead of just trying to place the girl across from him, the man seemed to suddenly perceive that he was being challenged.

"Lei é...?" he asked. "And you are...?" looking first at Paolo, then back to Nicki.

"Ah, signore, you don't know me. I'm Nicki, the waitress at Ristorante Girasole, Rita's place in Genoa." The man nodded slightly in recognition of the restaurant's name. "Rita said I could find you here, and that perhaps you could teach us something about *tartufi*."

With that the man sighed, not for want of knowledge about truffles, but as a sad reminder of the state of this year's harvest. Nicki introduced Paolo and the two newcomers were invited to sit at the old man's table.

"This is Edoardo," she said, looking at Paolo. "He is the smartest and most reliable *trifolào* in all of Piedmont.

At Nicki's extravagant description, a big grin spread across Edoardo's face and his head bobbed twice as if to rebuff – at least mildly – her compliments.

Nicki looked directly into Edoardo's eyes yet addressed Paolo, telling him how the old man had hunted truffles in the woods around Alba for many years. Edoardo's eyebrows lifted in an age-old Italian gesture to say, "yes, many years," but without admitting how many. Nicki went on to praise his skills, but mostly she focused on Edoardo's knowledge of the tuber, the ways of the *trifolài,* the market, and even the vagaries of pricing over the decades.

"What do you think has happened?" Nicki asked him directly. In a town where truffle is king, she knew everyone was talking about the harvest and she didn't have to elaborate.

Edoardo sighed again and looked down at wrinkled hands that he had wrapped gently around the warm cup of cappuccino on the table before him. He thought for a long time, as if he was processing all the information he had received in the preceding days, and he honestly wanted to explain to Nicki what he thought was the problem. He looked at her, mostly ignoring Paolo, and began with a very technical analysis.

"You know, the truffle is a strange thing. We have studied it for centuries, discovered the trees it likes to grow around, and fought with the right animals to harvest it." Edoardo continued to refer to the truffle as it, and seemed to be giving it a personality in the process.

"The white truffle is the most confusing of all," a comparison to the Périgord black truffle, what most gourmets considered the only challenge to the supremacy of Piedmont's *Tuber magnatum.* "It moves around and sometimes surprises us by turning up in the roots of trees that so far were not growing a crop. Then the next year, it disappears again."

Nicki waited patiently while Edoardo's mind ruffled through the scientific minutiae from wild harvest to the *tartufaie*, or truffle farms. Paolo sat rapt at the words, although there was so much information spilling out of Edoardo's mouth that he couldn't process or retain all of it.

"Most people think that oak and hazelnut trees are best, but those are not alone. The truffle is mischievous, and likes to have us wander the hills trying to find it. But don't bother the trees that have lots of brush and weeds at their base," Edoardo said, making the point that green growth at a trees foundation was usually a sign that no tubers would be found below.

Now he was wandering off into a world of his own, communing with the truffle rather than the two people who sat with him, and Nicki had to bring him back to the present.

"Edoardo, where have the truffles gone?"

"*Non so*," he said with a shrug, "I don't know," a confession was made with real emotion. "I don't know, but they can't be gone forever."

Paolo, warming to the conversation, now spoke. "Do you remember another year when there were so few truffles?"

Edoardo paused to consider this, staring off to a spot in the café that was somewhere behind Nicki. Again, he sighed, and said, "No. Never."

"And last year was good, si?" Nicki asked.

"*Si. L'anno scorso e' superbo!*" he replied with gusto.

All three exchanged glances across the table, a silent way of acknowledging that the facts don't fit. Alba couldn't have had a superb harvest last year and next to nothing this year. There was more to the story than met the eye, eyes which on Edoardo seemed now to be watering.

"We can't have lost it," he exclaimed with obvious sadness. From his earlier personalization of the truffle to the emotion he now demonstrated, it was clear that, to Edoardo, *tartufi* were a part of him and a part of the history and a part of the culture of this town.

33

PICKING AT THE SURFACE

Later in the day, Francesco found Alfonso at the Akash wine bar on Via Vittorio Emmanuele. His friend was sitting alone and staring at his wine glass, as if looking for answers to life's questions.

"What do you think you'll find in there?" he asked Alfonso.

Looking up, Alfonso shrugged his shoulders and just said, "Nothing," and looked down again.

Francesco sat down, still without drawing much of a reaction from Alfonso.

"Girlfriend problems, Alfie? She seems very nice. What's the problem?"

"It's not Lidia. I'm just worried about the truffles. They're gone, you know."

At this Francesco leaned in closer to his friend and pressed him for more information.

"You remember that bet we had a couple months ago, about the computer program?"

"Yeah," Francesco nodded.

"Well," Alfonso paused and gulped. "It works."

"Great. You can track people with the GPS chip in their phone. The police and phone company have been doing that for years."

"Yeah, I know," Alfonso said ruefully. "But they just track criminals and people under suspicion, right?"

Francesco leaned back and laughed. "I wish life was that simple. No, I doubt they only track criminals and people under suspicion."

Alfonso took a sip from his wine glass as the waiter finally approached to take Francesco's order.

"I'll have a glass of Nebbiolo," said Francesco, "and my friend here will have another."

"Si, signore," said the waiter as he retreated.

"People could use it for other purposes," Alfonso continued. "If they had the right cell numbers."

Francesco only nodded, but still didn't know where his friend was going.

"Are you trying to track someone, Alfie? Why? Who?"

Alfonso eyed him carefully, guiltily.

"Do you remember our debate that night weeks ago, over wine at Del Vino's?"

Francesco nodded, then chuckled, "Yes, well maybe no," as he laughed. "I think we had too much to drink that night. I don't remember many details."

"I said that all I needed was someone's cell number and I could track them from Rome to New York. Yeah, yeah, I know that was a stupid way to put it, but do you remember?"

Francesco knew his friend well. Alfonso was sometimes insecure and he liked to conjure up challenges to prove to people that he was a person to be reckoned with. On this day, Francesco saw this aspect of his friend come to the fore.

"Si, and you said you'd prove it if I gave you some cell numbers. I did," Francesco remarked, then paused and searched the sky for a memory of whose numbers he had given to Alfonso.

"I gave you my cell number, and Tino's, and Raffaelo's. Maybe somebody else."

"Roberto, Luigi, and Andrea," Alfonso filled in. "Notice anything about those names?"

"Yeah, they're all friends of mine. Of ours." Francesco held his look of confusion while the waiter returned with two more glasses of wine.

Alfonso leaned in a bit, which drew Francesco in with him.

"They're all sons of *trifolài*," he whispered.

Francesco stared at him for a moment, sighed lightly in thought, then leaped to his feet.

"What!"

"Sit down," Alfonso said, grabbing Francesco's sleeve to pull him back into the seat.

"You're not saying you tracked our friends to their truffle fields and robbed them?"

"No, of course I didn't, but…"

"But," Francesco interrupted, "there's another reason. There are a thousand reasons. People talk about a fungus, some parasite, even a government conspiracy…"

"And a thief," said Alfonso.

"This can't be," Francesco's voice almost warbled in distress. "You couldn't have caused all this."

"Not to put too fine a point on this, but you were egging me on. Saying I couldn't do it; daring me to try."

Alfonso proudly claimed that his program could track the movements of every phone he entered into it, which is to say all the best *trifolài* in Alba. And the program stored data about their movements, and highlighted any spot, with specific geographical coordinates, where the cell phone appeared to linger for more than two minutes.

"Who knows about your program?" Francesco asked.

"No one, *nessuno!*"

"What can be done?"

"Nothing, *nulla*," Alfonso replied with fateful finality. "Wait for it to pass, for everything to blow over. Maybe next year will be better."

With that dispiriting conclusion, the two sat in silence and drank their wine. But neither could dispel the thought that someone might have gotten hold of Alfonso's program and been the cause of all this trouble for Alba. And Alfonso had his own, very personal, suspicions.

34

QUIET DINNER IN SINALUNGA

At home on the farm in Sinalunga, the dinners were a bit quieter than in the past. Despite Dito's famous silence at the dinner table, Catrina noticed an even greater withdrawal with the absence of Paolo. Dito would occasionally glance at the chair left empty by Paolo, puff out a little grunt, then resume his meal.

Catrina kept up a mostly one-sided conversation, asking her husband about the vineyard and the prospects for next year. They both knew there would be little to say about the vines during winter, but Catrina didn't know what to talk about. During these lonely dinners, it occurred to her that for the better part of the preceding twenty years, most of her mealtime conversation was with her son, and now she had to acknowledge that her husband was too quiet for her satisfaction.

Dito was a man who provided for his family. He loved her and their son, and his behavior made it clear that nothing mattered more to him than their welfare. He just wasn't much of a conversationalist. Catrina pondered her new reality during dinner one night, and resolved to change their schedule to add some fun to their day.

"After we finish," she began, "let's go to Piazza Cavour for gelato."

"*Perche?*" was all Dito could think to say. "Why"

"Because I want to," Catrina said lightly, laying her hand on her husband's arm. And playing the part of a young coquette, she added, "Wouldn't you like to buy your wife some gelato?"

Dito grinned, and as he cocked his head to one side, it was obvious how much he loved this woman. He was a quiet, introverted man, and this woman who deserved so much had given her life to him. He didn't often show his affection, but he inwardly thanked the gods for bringing Catrina into his life. Fortunately, she knew this, and could see it at that moment in his eyes. A quiet man can't suddenly become an evocative one, so his reply was terse, but just what she wanted.

"*Certo,*" was all, "certainly."

Later that evening, while they walked the evening's *passeggiata* and enjoyed their gelato, they talked about Paolo. It seemed like that was the one subject that would bring Dito out a bit. He laughed at Catrina's stories, reminding him of Paolo's early years, and he described for his wife how hard their son worked in the vineyard.

"He worries," said Dito, "I know he does. He worries that I don't appreciate his effort. But I do."

"Well, maybe you should tell him."

With that, Dito nodded, but both of them knew that his quiet nature would prevent him from offering praise to his son.

"And if he doesn't come back?" Catrina asked.

It was clear that Dito didn't want to consider that possibility. He looked at his wife with a controlled sense of horror. He knew that Paolo would leave someday, probably when he got married; that was normal. But if he left for any other reason, well, that would be abnormal.

"He'll come back," he said.

"And you'll show you missed him?"

"Si," was all Dito would add, but he couldn't figure out how he would change his nature to keep his son closer, even given the chance.

35

LAST HARVEST

*I*t was about time. They had been working through the night for a week and half, making good progress he had to admit, but he had long since concluded that they had enough truffles for this plan.

In fact, the man was so sure they had enough that he began storing some for own use. And he had taken to asking questions in the market about how to prepare them and how long they lasted. The second question was what got him to stop hoarding the truffles he had unearthed.

"They're only fresh for about a week," said one storekeeper. He wouldn't be done with this plan for more than a week and, if the shopkeeper was right, all the truffles that the man had taken would be, what, "overripe?"

But it was his first question – how to prepare them – that got him in hot water with her.

"What are you doing, you idiot?" she said. "Don't go around Alba asking all these questions about how to prepare truffles when everyone's asking questions about where they all are."

After that they decided to end the hunt and call in the truck to get them out of the warehouse.

He never could figure out how she knew he was talking to shopkeepers. Must have eyes all around Alba. Gave him the creeps. He wondered what else she saw him doing.

"Idiot, huh! Bitch!"

36

A DEWY MORNING

It was early, and only the shopkeepers were out. They swept off the walkways in front of their stores, traded stories about last evening's commerce, and argued about soccer scores. The dew was slowly dissipating and the cool air of the morning was being warmed by the rising sun. It was a scene repeated in every great city built upon centuries of age. Towering cathedrals shouldered next to huddled newsstands and aromatic cafés. The cobblestones of ancient roads contributed their peculiar clack-clack as wagons and wheelbarrows rolled by, and early-rising pedestrians yawned and took in the sight, sounds, and smells of a venerable city.

Alfonso walked down the Via Bosio with purpose early that morning. He was not one to rise from bed so early, but today he found a special purpose in locating

Francesco. He knew he'd find him at the Caffé Revello on Piazza Cagnasso.

As he turned the corner, Alfonso quickly spied Francesco sipping his *gran café*.

"Buon giorno, Alfie," he said with a merry tone that morning brings.

"Buon giorno, Francesco."

Alfonso breezed past his friend to buy a double espresso at the cashier's desk. He watched Francesco out of the corner of his eye while waiting for the cashier to stamp the ticket and hand it to him, then glanced over at Francesco from the counter while waiting for the barista to prepare his drink.

Sitting down at Francesco's table, Alfonso took a direct and immediate approach to his subject.

"Your friends are trying too hard to figure out what happened to all the truffles."

"Si," replied Francesco, "even Nicki." Francesco's earlier cheery mood evaporated and his voice picked up an edge of concern.

"Make them stop, lose interest, whatever. If they try too hard, we may get drawn into it."

"Well," Francesco said, shifting in his chair uncomfortably. "We didn't really do anything, right?"

"Do you want to try to explain that to the magistrate when they find out about the program?"

Francesco looked at his friend doubtfully, then peered down into his coffee cup. Twisting it left, then right, he said, "No."

They spoke in somewhat muted voices for a few more minutes. Alfonso said the "investigation" – a word he repeatedly with his fingers making the symbol for quotations marks – is pointless and would just make everyone in Alba mad. He said they would never find anything.

"*D'accordo?*" asked Alfonso, "do we agree?"

Francesco sighed, looked into his friend's eyes, and nodded once more.

The morning coffee break took on an air of a cover-up, and it didn't escape Francesco's attention that Alfonso seemed almost to be sizing him up.

"There will be questions," Alfonso continued, "but the fewer the better. If your friends would just accept the situation, pay more for the truffles, and go back to Genoa, we would all be better off."

"But we are not involved," said Francesco.

Alfonso looked sideways at his friend as he sipped his coffee. Putting the cup down, he arched one eyebrow, as if to suggest doubt at Francesco's claim, and sighed.

"No, not in stealing truffles," was Alfonso brief summary, but his voice and excuse both sounded thin.

37

SOMEONE'S BEEN DIGGING HERE

Later that morning, Tomaso was in the piazza himself, selling the few truffles that were left in his field. There was great interest among the chefs and serious cooks in Alba, but the haggling began immediately after they heard the price.

"*E' troppo caro!*" complained one man who was already decked out in chef's toque. "It's too expensive!"

Tomaso lifted his shoulders and eyebrows in unison, and in apology, and struggled to explain the same reason he had given to so many others.

"There are so few *tartufi* this year, and I still must make some money. I have only one-third of last year's crop, so I should be charging three times as much to make up the difference, but I am not."

"No, but you are charging twice the price," the chef said, "and still it is too much!"

"Si, I understand you, but I don't know what I can do."

"Charge the same price as last year. We'll make wonderful food at the restaurant – although much less of it – and we'll make lots of fervent believers again. Then, next year, you'll have more and we can make more money then."

"But if I charge last year's price, I won't make enough money."

"And if I pay this year's price, I won't be able to sell the truffle dishes in the restaurant."

And so it went, one transaction after another. Most of these engagements Tomaso ended by compromising – some profit, some loss – but he was still dejected with each sale.

Bruno, who was also fighting a losing battle with buyers, waited for Tomaso to complete one of his sales, then approached him to talk about what he had found.

"I don't think it's a virus either, Tomaso."

Tomaso hadn't told Bruno what they had decided the day before, but let him speak.

"Ordinarily, we only go out at night," as if Bruno had to remind Tomaso, "so we can't really see how the earth has been disturbed in our truffle beds, right? Well, my crop has been so small, I had to look harder. So I went back during the day," a comment that drew worried looks from Tomaso, "and I found the earth around my hunting ground was disturbed."

The revelation didn't take Tomaso by surprise. He maintained his look of worry that Bruno would expose his fields to discovery by tending them during the day, but otherwise he accepted the news about the earth being disturbed without commenting.

Francesco approached his father and he heard only the last part of the conversation.

"Someone's been digging here," Bruno said. Francesco stopped at the words, and stood stone still.

38

TOO CLOSE FOR COMFORT

Alfonso was standing awkwardly at Akash Lounge, leaning uncomfortably against the countertop to order his drink. His scowl and constant shifting from his left foot to his right telegraphed his unease. Lidia was standing beside him, with her right hand on his back, leaning in.

"What's the matter, Alfie? Why are you so tense?"

"It's the truffles, damn truffles!" he said. "I can't believe this happened."

Her eyebrows bunched together and Lidia tried again.

"Everyone's worried, or mad," she began, "but why is it bothering you so?"

Just then, Francesco approached the couple and noticed Alfonso's agitation right away. He stood on his friend's other side and questioned him too.

"This is a great problem," Francesco said, "and we've got a problem, too. But I don't think we should say anything out here, where people can hear us. Let's let things smooth out."

Lidia stared keenly at Francesco, trying to read the thoughts behind his words.

Alfonso remained mostly quiet, uttering comments only in short bursts, as if trying to squeeze them in between periodic waves of emotion.

"Haven't even harvested the fruit. Haven't sold a thing. Gotta check the warehouse and see if anything's left."

Lidia shot Francesco a strange glance. Whatever he was talking about, Alfie seemed about ready to crack.

"Look, Alfie, maybe I can help," she said, "I need to talk to you. Would you excuse us, Francesco?"

With that, Francesco walked away toward the sidewalk café. He, too, needed a drink.

Lidia took Alfonso's arm and led him down the street toward her car, leaning in close and whispering to him along the way.

"You're talking about your produce and your fruit business," she commented. "Are you afraid you're losing your business?"

"No!" he nearly shouted, but Lidia pushed him into the car so they could avoid making a scene. "I'm worried about the truffles."

"But you were saying you hadn't even harvested yet, and you don't know if there's anything left," Lidia responded. "You have lots of the produce still in your warehouse," she said.

Alfonso cast a confused glance in her direction. He wondered when was Lidia at his warehouse.

"Let's go," she said. "We'll look over the inventory together and I'll show you that it's safe there."

He was standing in front of Ratti Elio's shop across the street from the Akash Lounge when he saw them emerge from the dim interior into the sunlight. The shopkeeper had just handed him a tagliatartufo, the tool he'd need later to shave the truffles that he kept for himself, and the shopkeeper was still talking to him as he stared at Lidia and Alfonso walking down the side street.

At one point the shopkeeper noticed that the man was distracted and stopped talking in mid-sentence. He had disregarded her instructions and was asking people on the street and in the shops about truffles. He was even getting a quick lesson in proper shaving thickness from this man, this man who was concerned about the truffle harvest yet oblivious to the thief standing right in front of him. It made him want to steal his tagliatartufo too, just to make a point.

But he didn't.

Instead, he watched Lidia guide Alfonso toward her car. He barely caught a single phrase... "in your warehouse."

39

HAULING IT AWAY

The two old mariners had been sitting around Barraccone too long. They felt they were getting soft. The only reason they put up with all this time on land was because they were getting paid by the day, and their real reward was still at the end of the journey.

"It's a good thing she's paying for this hotel," said the man with the stocking cap.

They spent their days mostly in and around that small town, but drove to Castiglione Falletto on occasion just to get away. They couldn't approach Alba, under strict instructions to avoid making an appearance there, but they found that Castiglione was small enough not to attract attention and there were a couple of nice places to eat there.

That morning, when she had called, they were sitting at Bar del Peso sipping their cappuccino and watching the workmen come and go. This was a popular place in the early hours. Many workers, some dressed in business attire and some in work clothes, passed through the door, hailed the lady behind the counter and often ordered "the usual." Fathers with children on the way to school and mothers pushing strollers passed this way.

The proprietor inside seemed to know them all, and know them well. That was the only thing that gave the seamen pause. She knew everyone who passed through her doors, so she might wonder who were these new "regulars" who came often but never spoke to her.

But they disregarded their concerns because the town was far removed from Alba, and Bar del Peso's position on the only intersection in Castiglione Falletto allowed them to watch the comings and goings of the place.

The man in the flannel hat pulled the phone from his pocket on the first ring.

"Pronto."

"It's time to get the truck and pick up the truffles at the warehouse."

"Where is this warehouse?" he asked.

"I put instructions on the seat of the truck. Be there this afternoon at four o'clock," and she hung up.

After hearing the click, the man stared at his cell phone for a moment, then slipped it back into his pocket.

40

PIAZZA ROSSETTI

Nicki and Paolo were prowling the streets listening to the scattered conversations. They knew only a few people in Alba – not like Rita and Stefano – so it was harder to approach just anyone to ask difficult questions about the truffle harvest. Nicki's confidence and resolve made her the obvious leader, and strangers more easily stopped to listen to this diminutive, though attractive, young woman, so Paolo remained at her shoulder and seldom spoke.

"I'm still confused," Paolo admitted. "If last year was so good, and the years before that were good, what has changed? Is there a virus, a thief, or what?"

Nicki considered the question, but had no answers. Thieves can't steal the truffles, because no thief would know how to find them. "That's the point of harvesting at night," she reminded Paolo. But it would have to be a virulent strain of bacteria to wipe out most of the crop in a single year.

For a while, they mingled with the pedestrians, chefs, and *trifolài* who crowded the Via Vittorio Emanuelle before noon. Nicki listened intently to the conversations around them while Paolo tried to keep his attention on truffle traffic while enjoying the young beauties who were part of every Italian streetscape. "*La bella figura*," the Italian phrase that needed little translation, was on display in Alba on that sunny morning.

Nicki turned to ask him something and, picking up on his distraction, she elbowed Paolo with a grin. "Stay with me here, Romeo," she said.

"If we accompanied some of the hunters tonight, we would know more," she suggested.

"But I thought you said no one would let us come along."

"Probably not, but do you think I could talk them into it?" she asked.

Nicki gave no hint of using her alluring smile as bait, although Paolo almost suggested it.

"Maybe," he admitted, "but who would do it?"

"We could call Edoardo and see if knew someone who would let us."

Without hesitation, Nicki drew out her cell phone and punched in the number for Edoardo.

"Would one of the *trifolài* let us go along tonight so we can get a better understanding?"

"Understanding of what?" Edoardo asked, not masking his suspicion. "Hunting for *tartufi*, or hunting for thieves?"

Nicki ignored his direct reference to thieves, but replied, "Of course, the truffles. Rita and Stefano will be back soon and they'll want to know – we all want to know – how to solve this puzzle."

Edoardo rubbed his chin and paused for a long time considering this. It was clear that he wanted to help, but he was checking his mental directory to come up with a name of someone who would cooperate.

"*Nulla,*" he said, "nothing." Nicki paused to give Edoardo a moment to reconsider, but then kindly thanked him. They exchanged goodbyes, and then hung up.

While Nicki thought this over, Paolo easily saw the next step.

"Why don't you ask Francesco? Either he or his father would let us go along, right?"

"Surely," she answered. "I'll talk to him tonight."

They passed by a young couple talking in whispers. Paolo expected love talk in such subdued tones, but the anxious look on the woman's face discounted this.

"I don't know what happened," she said, "That's all I've heard."

"Dead bodies," her partner responded with muted alarm. Then relaxing some, "It's just part of the whole medieval atmosphere they're trying to create for the Palio and the truffle season."

"Yeah," said the young woman, "That's it."

Paolo and Nicki continued down the street but heard an older man, obviously a local farmer, confiding in whispered tones with his companion. They couldn't make out the words, but the conversation between the two men seemed ominous.

41

THE WAREHOUSE

The morning chill had lost its edge and, with it, the fog that blanketed this area in the fall had burned off. The two seamen returned to their hotel rooms and doffed the heavier clothes, knowing that this afternoon would bring work and, with it, sweat.

They drove the identified route which took them down well-used roads, through factory areas, and into the farmland. At the foot of the hills, where the trees gathered more closely than on the plain, they turned right onto a rough gravel road and followed it for a few miles.

As the gravel gave way to dirt, the ruts in the road became more pronounced, and the men shifted side to side as the truck bucked with each exposed root and fallen branch that they drove over. Around a curve to the left and standing somewhat clear of the trees was a warehouse that had wires running to it to provide electricity but little else in the way of civilized convenience.

They backed the truck up to the warehouse, unlocked the door and stepped inside. The front room was small, with only a desk, file cabinets and the usual furnishings of an office. Off to one side there were large doors, at least twelve feet high, with large stainless steel handles. Pulling on the handles, the doors swung outward reluctantly. They were heavy, and the hinges seemed to be undersized for the task.

Inside the doors hung long strips of rubber, each about one foot wide, but hung individually so a person could push between strips and enter. Which they did.

There in the refrigerated room they found sacks and sacks piled up in the corner. But even the burlap of the bags could not contain the aromas that exuded from the heap. Even for two grizzled men of the sea, the aroma brought smiles to their faces. Then, their eyes growing accustomed to the dimmer light, they saw it in the other corner.

They looked at each other with expressionless faces, but the one in the felt cap pulled the cell phone from his pocket, flipped it open, and punched in a few numbers.

"*Pronto*," came a woman's voice.

"What do we do with the guy in the corner?"

"Leave him." Lidia's voice took on a steely edge, an edge she was careful to disguise when talking to Alfonso and his clueless friends in Alba.

Flipping the cover shut on the phone and exchanging one more glance, the two men set to work carrying the bundles of truffles out to the waiting truck, under the black lifeless gaze of the man in the corner with a dried stream of blood staining his left cheek.

Once the haul was completed and the refrigerated room stood empty, they locked the door to the warehouse and pulled silently out of the drive onto the dirt road they had come in on. By her instructions, though, they followed a slightly different route and climbed a gentle hill deeper into the trees on the mountain. Only about fifteen minutes along, they saw the landmark she had mentioned, a tall outcropping of granite that stood next to the road, and they pulled to a stop.

Lidia emerged from behind the rock with a box large enough to require two hands. She thanked them for their help, said she had their payment but that the other box with Euros was still "back there," as she indicated by tossing her head back in the direction of the rocks.

As the men circled the granite stand to retrieve their payment, she followed them. They turned and stood face-to-face with the handgun she held.

"You've been very helpful and I couldn't have done it without you," she said and without hesitation she put two bullets in each of them in quick succession. Approaching their bodies sprawled on the ground, she put one more bullet in each man's head.

What the seamen failed to notice, or didn't have time to consider, were the shallow graves that were already dug just feet from where their bodies now lay. So with little effort, the woman dragged their bodies that short distance, rolled them over into the soft earth, and covered each with dirt, then wet leaves, then a scattering of broken branches.

Lidia went to the truck, pulled one wire off the distributor cap and replaced it with a burned out wire, then retreated to her own car and drove away. The gun was tossed out of the car as she drove over a bridge covering a primitive-looking ravine, an overgrown rift in the earth that didn't look like it had witnessed human traffic in centuries.

42

LOSING FAITH

*I*t was time for the truffles to be moved, that he knew, and the smuggler suspected that she had someone hired to handle the chore. She always had strings of employees working for her, each with only a small piece of the puzzle, so no one knew enough to cause her trouble.

Funny thing, though, her employees always seemed to disappear. He knew that; why didn't they?

So he needed to track her to her next destination, but he knew this next chapter of the plan was taking place in the deep woods, so there would be no way for him to keep close without her hearing his rental car or reacting to some movement along the trail.

But he knew the men she was going to meet would be coming from the warehouse that he had worked so hard to fill. So instead of following her, he decided to hide out near the warehouse and follow them. Dumb old men; they'd never be able to pick up the scent.

They arrived on schedule, as instructed, spent nearly two hours loading the sacks, although he thought they could have worked faster. Just when the big fat one fired up the engine of the old truck, he started his own car. Then he drove behind, carefully behind, and watched their turns from the roadside before following.

The truck was old enough to make more noise than his car did; so with his windows open in the October air, he could hear them far up ahead. Until the rumbling sounds of the truck engine suddenly choked to a stop.

He stopped his car, climbed out of the driver's seat and tip-toed up behind them. There were many autumn leaves on the ground so he had to pick his steps carefully, but he got to a small clearing just as he heard a "pop-pop" sound, followed by another "pop-pop." The man hid behind a tree and saw her standing over two bodies, then he watched as she put another bullet into each of them. He turned around and tip-toed back out instead of waiting.

He let his car coast down the hillside road for a few hundred yards before starting the engine. Just as he did, he heard the low rumble of another car behind. He pulled quickly into a forested drop-off on the right, and dug back in far enough to be concealed. Just in time.

She rolled past in her car. "Must have left the truck up the hill," he thought, and wondered whether he should retrieve it himself and abandon her, but thought better of it. She didn't leave loose ends. If he went up the hill, something bad was bound to happen.

When the sound of car had disappeared down the hillside, he pulled his car out and started down.

43

PALIO DEGLI ASINI

About two o'clock on Sunday afternoon, large crowds began to drift in the direction of the Piazza Cagnasso where the Palio degli Asini would be run. The permanent bleachers were augmented by additional stands to handle the crowd at Alba's biggest celebration of the year.

All day, parades of costumed actors had marched through the streets, announcing their approach with trumpets and drums, dressed in the colors of their *borgo*, or neighborhood.

The donkeys and riders assembled on the oval track as the crowds filled the stands. The donkeys established early that they would decide when to go and when to stop, even which direction to go if they chose.

Every race has winners and losers, and usually the results matter. The *borghi* of Alba no doubt cared about the results of this race too, but all was done in good sport and backs were slapped and jokes were told at everyone's expense.

The Palio degli Asini was completed and the crowds began to draw out of the stands, while the costumed "royal family" departed under the sound of trumpets. Nicki and Paolo slipped out of the bleachers too, and joined the throngs now moving toward the streets of Alba.

"Did you see Bruno and Giorgio in the stands?" asked Paolo.

"Si, I'm sure they enjoy the Palio too."

"And many of the truffle hunters we've met," he continued.

At first, Nicki didn't get his point, but then realized that even the truffle market seemed to be suspended during the festivities.

"Again, not too surprising," she said.

"True," Paolo said thoughtfully, everyone was here, except Alfonso and Lidia."

"How can you tell in this crowd?" Nicki asked.

"I told Alfonso we'd meet at Caffè Rossetti before the race, but he never showed up," Paolo said.

That struck Nicki as strange, since Paolo was not very friendly with Alfonso.

"Why meet with him?"

"Well, actually, I was more interested in Lidia, and I thought I could talk to Alfonso and find out more about her," was Paolo's reply.

Nicki seemed even more confused.

"I still don't understand. Why do you want to find out about Lidia?"

"Something's not right, and I don't trust her. I think Alfonso's been acting strange, and I think she has something to do with it," he continued. "Besides, where's Francesco?"

At that, Nicki's face burned red, since Francesco was supposed to meet her at the Palio and didn't, and she hoped that Paolo would not bring it up.

"So, Lidia, Alfonso, and Francesco are among the few people in Alba who didn't attend the race," he said. "Doesn't that make you curious?"

Nicki looked at Paolo, her eyelids drooping in a way that someone does when facing disappointment and uncertainly, but she only turned and walked toward the side street with a determined stride.

"It's Antonio," she heard from someone standing in the doorway of a bakery at the edge of the Piazza Cagnasso.

"No, please, no," exclaimed a woman in an apron, soiled from a day of tossing loaves of bread.

Out of curiosity, Nicki stopped to listen, and Paolo was right behind her.

"What is it?" he asked.

"Shhh," was her terse reply, which she said without taking her eyes off of the couple at the bakery doorstep.

"What happened?" the aproned woman asked of her companion.

"*Non so,*" he said, shrugging his shoulders. "His son came to the farm, looking for his father. Then he saw the dirt in the barn turned over, carelessly, like someone was digging for something."

He paused, then added ruefully, "Or burying something."

"He dug around it with his zappino, then used the shovel, till he struck something."

"Oh, no," she cried. His son, Carlo, he didn't find his father's body, did he?" she asked, hoping the answer would stop the twisting feeling she had in her stomach.

The man looked at her for a moment, then down at the pavement, and only nodded his head.

"Si, Antonio, and their dog, buried together in the barn."

44

THE SECRET STARTS TO UNFOLD

Alba was caught up in the revelry of the Palio and that evening everyone was retelling stories of the race. The costumed parades resumed after the Palio and street scenes resembled something from the 16th century. Lords and ladies proceeded past restaurants and sidewalk cafés, fools and thieves were dragged roped together by their wrists, and trumpets blared to clear the path.

It didn't seem to matter which *borgo* won the Palio. At least, Paolo couldn't tell which one had, since all the groups that marched down Via Vittorio Emanuelle that evening seemed to be as full of cheer as the last one.

By evening, Francesco had joined up with Nicki and Paolo, and he walked down the sidewalk at Nicki's side.

Paolo wandered off, his attention spent on searching the crowds for pretty girls.

Nicki was quiet for a time, then said matter-of-factly, "I thought the rider on Bruto was the best," making small observations to pretend interest.

"No," countered Francesco, with the confidence of being a former rider himself. "Piccolo was best," referring to the donkey that had bested the field coming around the last curve, only to quit the race in favor of munching on the pot of fresh flowers at the gate.

Nicki peered for an uncomfortable time into Francesco's eyes, who sought to avoid her gaze.

"Where were you today," she asked, with an evident tinge of anger in her voice.

"I was at my father's farm," he replied, but didn't try to explain further.

Nicki switched subjects, and explained to Francesco her idea about investigating the truffle problem. "We could interview as many *trifolài* as we can, take notes, and ask them how much the crop has dropped since last year. Maybe, by charting where the hunter works and how much he lost, we might discover whether it's a virus, a thief, or something else. Could I go out on a hunt with you tonight?"

Francesco listened with some interest, but showed some doubt.

"No, no," he replied thoughtfully. "The hunters always try to avoid the *fisco*, the government tax man, so they won't admit anything about their harvest. And even if they were willing to tell you how much they lost this year, they won't let you go on a hunt. Their grounds are secret."

"And what about hunting with you?" she repeated.

Francesco appeared slow to reply. It was a combination of tradition that made only men truffle hunters and a reluctance to let Nicki become even more involved. With that thought, he recalled Alfonso warning that they had to tamp down the investigation of this problem. So he didn't answer her.

Nicki stared directly at him, waiting for a response as they walked down the via. Nothing was offered by Francesco, and Nicki retreated to a sullen silence.

At the corner, they saw Paolo talking to Giorgio, the *trifolào*, with their heads close together as if trying to keep their conversation from being overheard. Francesco looked down at the cobblestones, pausing instead of moving forward, but Nicki wanted to find out what Paolo was learning. Seeing them approach, Giorgio turned to the couple and welcomed them into the conversation.

"I was just telling Paolo, here, that Edoardo thinks there has been a great theft."

"Yeah," said Nicki, "that's what everyone thinks," and as if on reflex, she cast a suspicious eye toward her boyfriend.

After a bit more conversation, mostly covering ground each of them had already dug through, Francesco was showing signs of giving in to his annoyance with Nicki. He complained that she was spending too much time trying to find the truffles, the same complaint he raised with Paolo that morning at the hotel.

Paolo listened to Giorgio, and Nicki's questioning during the conversation, but he also kept an eye on Francesco whose body language suggested a growing discomfort with the trend of the discussion. In fact, Paolo's silence during the conversation even got Nicki's attention at one point, causing her to glance over at Francesco, who was standing idly by, acting as if he wished the conversation would soon end so he could move on. Paolo now suspected that Francesco knew more than he was telling.

Turning her attention to Francesco, Nicki said, "Rita and Stefano left us in Alba to find out more. Why aren't you more concerned?" Her words eerily recalled Paolo's own that morning.

"Your father is a *trifolào*, you are a *trifolào*," she continued, as if accusing him of betraying his heritage.

"My father is a farmer, and if the fates decide so, I will be also," Francesco fired back. "Hunting for truffles is a noble activity, but it's not an occupation. I do care," he emphasized his point, "but we can't live on truffles."

Paolo listened with some detachment, knowing this quarrel was spurred a bit by the relationship between Nicki and Francesco and not just the truffles, and yet he disagreed with a part of Francesco's last comment. It's true the *trifolài* couldn't live on their profits from selling the little tuber, but Alba certainly lives on its reputation.

A chill air filled the space between Nicki and Francesco as Paolo looked on.

45

WHAT NOW?

*H*e knew she'll be thrilled – thrilled! – to hear that the hunter's body had been discovered. Actually, he was a bit nervous himself. He didn't like loose ends either. But as before, he had trouble separating his concern about the dead body from his fear of her.

"Yeah, I already heard," was how she started in when he called her.

"Kind of stupid, right?" she continued.

"No," he responded, defensively. He wasn't going to let her just walk over him; he was going to fight back.

"Well," she spat out, "what now?"

"I don't really care," the man began, weakly, but he was trying to build a case. "He's dead, so what? Maybe they'll think he's the one who stole the damn truffles, and he was murdered because of it."

This sounded crazy before he even finished saying it. Her long silence on the phone made it clear that she agreed, and that she was really pissed off.

"You've got to leave. Now"

"That's ridiculous," her partner blurted out. "There's no connection between the truffles, the hunter, and us. Besides, we're almost done here."

"You are done here," she said with finality.

He protested lamely. Although her silence made it clear that she wasn't going to change her mind, the man decided he wasn't bound by her, or their partnership. He would decide for himself.

46

LA TERRAZZA DA RENZA

The first sound Paolo heard that morning was his *telefono*, perched fortunately right next to his bed in Locanda Cortiletto d'Alba.

"*Pronto*," he said, the Italians' typical phone greeting.

"Paolo," came a woman's voice. Still half asleep, Paolo couldn't place a name with the voice, although he guessed it was either his mother or Zia Rita.

"Paolo," came the voice again. By now Paolo was awake, at least enough to recognize his aunt's voice.

"*Si, Zia Rita. Buona mattina*," he said, "good morning."

"Actually," she corrected, "it's near midday." But her chiding was accompanied by a discernible humor, as Rita had come to know Paolo's sleep pattern.

"What is happening up there," Rita queried.

Sitting up in bed and scratching his scalp, Paolo yawned before answering. "Nothing much. We have asked many of the *trifolài* what they think happened. The talk all over Alba is about the truffle harvest, and how the crop is down and the price is up. And we talked to Edoardo…" Here he paused as if suddenly remembering something.

"Oh, yeah," he said as he emerged from his near-sleep state. "Edoardo wants us to visit him today because he found something."

It was Monday, the day after the Palio, and Alba was quieter than on most days of the year. Since the Palio was a central event in the city, the "morning after" produced a collective hangover that would permeate the town.

"We're coming back up today," said Rita. "We'll arrive by train about five o'clock in the afternoon. When are you meeting with Edoardo?"

"For lunch. We'll be back in Alba by the time you arrive."

"D'accordo," she said. "We can meet at Cortiletto d'Alba around six."

Paolo flipped the phone closed, yawned again and stood to stretch his back. He had just turned toward the shower when a knock came at the door. He opened it and stepped back in surprise at his visitor.

"Ciao." Francesco stood before him, showered and dressed, a fact that made Paolo a bit embarrassed, but he let him enter the room.

"Why does Nicki care so much about the truffles?" Francesco asked. His annoyance at Nicki's questioning had grown since the day before, and Paolo was sensing a significant rift between the two young people.

"Nicki wants to know because the loss bothers her. Rita wants to know for the restaurant, so does Stefano. And I want to know because I'm discovering how much *tartufi* mean to the people of Alba. The better question is, why don't you want to know?"

Francesco peered at him momentarily, his eyes growing cold, and then he breathed deeply before letting out a long sigh. Calling on his family business, Francesco said, "Of course I want to know. My father is a *trifolào*, and I am training to take his place. Why wouldn't I want to know?"

Paolo was not apt to accept such a weak defense.

"So," Paolo replied, "what do you want?" After the words escaped his mouth, Paolo realized that they were not the most polite. But he decided not to retract them or rephrase them.

Again, Francesco looked at his feet. The gesture was one now recognized by Paolo as vintage Francesco. Observing it in other settings, Paolo knew that Francesco did this whenever he wanted to hide his feelings, or shield his eyes from view in order to mask what he was about to say.

"I want to find the truffles, but we're not going to find them by badgering the *trifolài* every day."

"Do you want to go to the *polizia*?" Paolo asked.

"No, no," Francesco said emphatically.

"What then?"

Acting defeated, Francesco just shrugged his shoulders, adding, "What's the use of seeing Edoardo today?"

"He wants to see us. Edoardo knows of our interest, he respects the measure of our concern, and he is heart-and-soul connected to the most famous product of Alba."

"Barolo," Francesco muttered.

"What?" asked Paolo, not hearing the single word response from Francesco.

"I said Barolo!" Francesco nearly spat the word out, letting his anger overwhelm him. "Barolo is more famous than truffles."

"Maybe," Paolo conceded, "but Alba wouldn't be Alba without the white truffle."

Francesco turned to leave; Paolo shut the door behind him and prepared for the day.

About an hour later, they met outside the hotel. Nicki was even more beautiful than before, wearing a flower-print sun dress that showed off her figure, and her eyes sparkled with what Paolo assumed was the excitement of the day's plans.

"No, Paolo," she corrected. "It's because I am anxious to show you the little town of Castiglione Falletto." She smiled brightly at Paolo while saying this, knowing that Francesco was standing just a few feet away.

With this she linked her right arm through Paolo's as Francesco fumed over being overlooked by her. Nicki knew full well what she was doing, and how this slight would affect Francesco, but she wasn't doing it for spite. She was still mad at him for not caring more about the plight of the truffle harvest, and her patience was growing thin.

For his part, Francesco decided to remain a part of the trio. Leaving them now might be a salve for his ego, but he felt a growing need to accompany them in their quest to uncover evidence of the a crime – a prospect that made Francesco increasingly uneasy.

Getting out of Alba is always tricky, as it is in most of the ancient citics of Italy. But once outside the city proper, the road to Castiglione Falletto straightened out and, in just about twenty minutes, they had arrived at the outskirts of the tiny town that was their destination.

So small was Castiglione Falletto that only a few streets dissected the town. In addition to an ancient castello – what medieval Italian town didn't have one? – there were only about three restaurants and a handful of shops. Francesco pulled quickly up to the curb just above a sharp decline in the roadway, alongside La Terrazza da Renza. It was the most quaint of the restaurants in the town, and the friendliest. Renza, the owner, was a portly woman whose excellent menu was respected by eager diners from a large area beyond Castiglione Falletto's borders.

The three walked from the car to the terrace overlooking the Piedmontese countryside.   Edoardo was ensconced in a corner table. He surveyed the terrace from this perch in a way that clearly conveyed that this was his table. As an elderly gentleman, a famous *trifolào*, and a venerated member of the town, such premier status would be expected. However, the restaurant still wouldn't have assumed this was "Edoardo's table" if he had not routinely graced their dining room and left handsome tips to go with his meals.

"*Buon giorno*," he said, opening his arms in a gesture of welcome but without rising. As the elderly statesman in truffle craft, he didn't have to rise to greet the visitors. While he seemed quiet and a bit secretive in Bottega del Caffè in Alba, in territory that was less like his home, here in Castiglione Falletto he behaved very much like the mayor of the town. The change in behavior was so remarkable that Paolo even wondered whether Signor Edoardo was, in fact, the mayor.

They each ordered from the menu, complementing their dishes with two bottles of wine – a white Arneis and a bottle of Gattinara, a red wine made from nebbiolo, the same grape which yielded Barolo from more selective vineyards.

They exchanged pleasantries for a few moments while getting the meal going, then Edoardo surprised them by bluntly stating that he believed the truffles had been stolen.

"*Sono stati rubati.*" he said.

Nicki was shocked. She had heard other rumblings, but dismissed them. But to hear Edoardo say this, well…

"*Perche?*" Francesco asked, almost to rebuff Edoardo's studied opinion.

"Because," Edoardo began, but paused for effect, "there's no sign of a virus."

"How do you know this," Paolo interjected.

With a proud smile, Edoardo sat back in his chair. "I have many contacts in this business. You forget who I am." He proceeded to explain how he was allowed to accompany some of the *trifolài* to their fields, where he took soil and truffle samples and marked the location. These samples he delivered to the agricultural labs, who analyzed them.

"The scientists are sure there is no virus," he reported, but with a glint of mischief in his eyes Edoardo added, "but they learned more about the type of soil and progress of the truffle by doing this."

With Paolo's agricultural upbringing, and the rush of information about truffles that he devoured since arriving in Alba, he absorbed much about the management and growth of truffles through reading the books about

DICK ROSANO

local culture that generously adorned each room in the Cortiletto d'Alba hotel. From his reading, he knew that different types of trees produced different types of truffles, so it was no surprise that the soil could have an effect also.

And he knew that mycologists had studied truffle culture for decades, with some success unraveling the mystery of the fungus. So hearing Edoardo claim that more had been discovered was both intriguing and a bit surprising, but Paolo was not about to question the *maestro di tartufi*!

"But how could they be stolen?" Francesco persisted.

"*Non so,*" Edoardo admitted, "I don't know." His earlier bravura proclamation lost some of its credibility since Edoardo had nothing to offer as proof. Francesco stared off into space, Nicki seemed lost in thought, and Paolo focused on Edoardo, sensing that there was something unsaid.

"But you seem so sure the *tartufi* were stolen. But you have no idea how?"

Edoardo emptied his wine glass as all eyes turned to him.

"It's just that *tartufi* don't just stop growing. I've been pulling these little diamonds from the ground for seventy years, and my father did so for fifty years before me. They've always been there, and they were there last year. How can they just not be there today? There must be *ladri*, thieves, at work here."

Paolo noticed the slightest flinch in Francesco, a twitch in his left cheek that couldn't be hidden. He couldn't process it, but decided that this was a disturbing sign from his tablemate. What did Francesco know about truffles and thieves?

47

RISTORANTE DELL'ENZO

After a slow awakening, by afternoon the city was teeming with people, as if the spectators and riders had recovered from the previous night's reverie and were ready for another day to celebrate the truffle festival. Sidewalk cafés were full – even between meals – shops were doing a brisk business, crowds roamed the piazzas and side streets, and glass clinked here and there among the cafés with tired feet giving in to thirsty mouths.

Paolo and Nicki spent the morning questioning restaurant owners and *trifolài* on the piazze, but they didn't learn anything new. They walked the city and talked about their lives., Paolo stood five inches taller than Nicki and when she was on one of her long narratives about life in Italy, she would occasionally look up at him for emphasis. From this angle, her eyelashes seemed longer than usual, adding an alluring accent to her already radiant face.

With the possible exception of her sister, Nicki didn't remember spending so much time talking and sharing life's secrets with anyone as she was doing with Paolo. The investigation that Rita and Stefano had left them to pursue – with its numerous dead ends and clueless responses – created an abundance of dead time that Nicki and Paolo filled with shared stories of their childhood, families, and life experiences.

Francesco saw them walking past the church on Piazza Risorgimento that afternoon and drew near. Nicki offered a cool "hello," but nothing more.

"Rita and Stefano are coming back today. Are you joining us for dinner tonight, right?" she asked.

Francesco paused to consider the "right" answer, wondering if the question was meant to elicit a "yes" or a "no," but then he nodded.

"Si," he said, a warble of guilt fluttering in his throat, "and papa will also be there."

Francesco sensed a strain between himself and Nicki, a problem he blamed on the truffledisappearance.

Nicki and Paolo made their way back to Cortiletto d'Alba to take a short afternoon break. Paolo had already retrieved his key from behind the desk and Nicki approached the clerk to request hers. With the key, the clerk handed her a note which Nicki read on the way to her room.

"We arrive this afternoon. Let's meet at Ristorante dell'Enzo for dinner at eight o'clock." It was signed by Rita, although Nicki hardly needed the reminder.

At the appointed time, they met at Enzo's, Paolo and Nicki walking from the hotel and Rita and Stefano appearing out of the crowd on the street at the same time. The interior of dell'Enzo's was slightly dimmed and soothing, with white tablecloths covering the tables, chairs of dark wood, a broad expanse of bar sporting about a dozen stools, and a colorful array of bottles decking out the backdrop. A refined grace permeated the room and soft tunes of Italian crooners filled the air.

A middle-aged man appeared, sized up the group and directed them to a table for four.

"*Ma, signore,*" began Stefano, "there will be two more." With that, the host spun on his heel, found another table near the window with more room, and quickly arranged the settings on the table to accommodate six people. As he cradled unneeded glasses and table cards, he leaned into the guests and waited for a preliminary order.

"*Il menu, per favore*," Rita said while she lowered herself into the chair. "A bottle of l'acqua minerale, and a bottle of Cavalotto Freisa." It was clear that Rita had her heart set on a big meal, skipping right past her usual choice of white wine to start and ordering one of Piedmont's very pleasant reds. It was also clear that this would not be the last of the wines to grace the table that night, and starting with Freisa presaged a move up to something big, no doubt Barolo.

Tomaso appeared in the doorway, scanned the room, and found the table of his friends. He started toward them as Francesco entered behind him.

"*Buona sera*," he said, with hugs and kisses for Nicki and Rita and heartfelt handshakes for the men. "*Come state?*" he added, "how are you?"

"*Bene, grazie, ma ho fame*," Stefano replied, rubbing his stomach to emphasize that he was hungry.

Francesco greeted the table as his father had, and then sat next to Nicki. By accident, Paolo occupied the seat on her other side; as such, both men's conversations would be passed in front of Nicki throughout the meal.

Rita carried her excitement onto the subject of food generally, and truffles specifically. She seemed energized by the return from Genoa, and was more animated that night than when they saw her last. First, she reported to Paolo that she had spoken to his mother who asked about his welfare, which prompted Nicki to smile and squeeze his cheek to mimic what she was sure his mother would do. He brushed her hand away but had to smile at the attention.

Rita also reported that Ristorante Girasole was doing great business and that everyone was eagerly awaiting the truffles.

Stefano interrupted her to tell how the guests at the restaurant were also anxious about the sudden disappearance of Nicki, then he smiled and looked at her in admiration.

Rita smiled too, but sometimes wondered why Italian men have to flirt with young women so openly. Shrugging her shoulders, and dispatching with her husband's interruption, Rita returned to the subject of the *tartufi*.

"You think they're anxious about losing Nicki; wait till our customers find out they're missing their truffles!" She threw an apologetic glance at Nicki, not wanting to compare her to a delicious morsel.

"What are the Albese saying?" Rita asked Tomaso.

"Everyone has their own idea, mostly rumors. Thieves, viruses," Tomaso began. "The rumor I like best is the one about a government conspiracy to punish the *trifolài* for tax-dodging by destroying the crop."

"Hmpph," muttered Stefano. "Italian governments change over every few months, but if they tampered with the *tartufi*, they'd be executed before they had a chance to resign."

Nicki looked at Francesco, expecting him to reveal what Edoardo had asserted earlier that day, but he just stared at his plate and seemed reluctant to speak. After waiting for him to take the lead, she turned back to the table and addressed Tomaso.

"Edoardo said he thinks the truffles have been stolen."

Tomaso knew Edoardo well, as did all serious truffle hunters, and no one doubted his wisdom.

"How does he know this?" he asked.

"Well, that's the problem," began Nicki. "He has no proof, but he has dismissed all other possibilities. And he only laughs at the government conspiracy theory."

Everyone at the table chuckled at this, and scattered comments recalled Stefano's earlier sentiment. Italians view their government with suspicion, but also with the patience a parent shows a child. The bureaucrats aren't thought of as evil, simply unskilled, so how would such a gaggle of incompetents be able to pull off a diabolical plot such as this?

Tomaso spied a friend and scientific ally, Riccardo, eating alone at the bar, and waved him over. Just as the waiter returned with the bottle of mineral water and Freisa, Riccardo, who is a mycologist by education and training, came toward the table. By Tomaso's urging, Riccardo squeezed another chair among the six at the table, eliciting groans from the waiter who now must bring back a table setting he had just removed.

"Riccardo Cuneo, you know Francesco," Tomaso began, and Riccardo and Francesco exchanged greetings. Following protocol, Tomaso introduced Rita and Stefano next, and the three shared polite handshakes. Then Tomaso introduced Paolo as Rita's nephew.

Displaying a theatrical flair, and knowing that the paunchy, middle-aged Riccardo wanted most to be introduced to the prettiest girl at the table, Tomaso paused for affect, then introduced Nicki.

"*Mi piacere*," Riccardo said with affection, reaching across the table to warmly take her hand, "my pleasure." Nicki was gracious and appreciative of the attention, but was also eager to show that she had more than beauty to offer this table.

"As I was telling everyone just before you arrived, Signor Cuneo..."

"*No, per favore*," Riccardo waved his hand to dismiss her words, "I am Riccardo. Hearing Signor Cuneo, especially from you, makes me feel old."

Continuing, Nicki said, "Okay, so, anyway, Edoardo told us this afternoon that he is convinced that the truffles have been stolen. What do you think, Signor..., *scusi*, Riccardo?"

"Of course, yes, of course," he began. Riccardo looked the part of a university professor, which he was, and he appeared to be gathering steam for a lecture on the mycology of the white truffle.

"As we all know, *Tuber magnatum* is an elusive treasure. It reappears in roughly the same spots each year, but with varying intensity and concentration. And sometimes the spots themselves may change."

Sure enough, his answer to Nicki's question was beginning to sound like a scholarly paper.

"The *tartufi* last year were abundant, and generally appeared exactly where the *trifolài* expected them to be. But this year, they didn't."

Looks were exchanged around the table, each diner wondering why Riccardo was describing, in such detail, what everyone in Alba – or all over Piedmont – already knew.

The waiter approached the table with a tray of antipasti. No one had ordered it but in this establishment it came with the meal. There were piles of aromatic olives, layer upon layer of roasted red peppers, herb-scented grilled eggplant, several types of cheese, and marinated mushrooms. With a clatter of plates, the waiter passed out the service to each place, retrieved serving pieces from his back pocket, and then made a slight turn to his left. Glancing back at the table before departing, he saw that the wine bottle was empty and said, simply, "*Un'altra?*"

"Si," said Stefano, knowing that with seven people at the table, another bottle of Freisa would be needed before embarking on the grand wine of the evening.

"Edoardo approached me at the lab to ask about viruses." With this statement, Riccardo regained everyone's interest, although by now he had to share their attention with the delectable appetizers on the platters before them.

"He asked whether we could decide if there was a virus or something, a fungus on a fungus, if you will." Riccardo laughed at his own joke but elicited only polite smiles from those chewing through their food.

Between bites, Tomaso expressed his opinion that there was, in fact, a virulent pest that could lay the harvest in *le Langhe* to waste. He had barely expressed this fear when, in his excited suspicions, he worried aloud whether the centuries-old tradition of truffle excellence was in jeopardy.

"*No, non c'e problema,*" Riccardo said, "there's no problem." Continuing on, Riccardo explained that his studies and tests – and he reminded the gathered guests that Edoardo had brought him both soil and truffle samples – had found no evidence of virus or bacteria or other pest.

Idly sampling some of the roasted pepper, Paolo inwardly wondered what Riccardo had done with what was left of the truffle "samples." Observing his corpulent physique, Paolo doubted that this mycologist would dispose of them other than in a consumable preparation.

They each contributed their own thoughts, between bites, while the waiter returned with another bottle of

Freisa. He distributed the entire contents of the bottle among the seven glasses, topped off their water glasses, and stood waiting for instructions.

In Piedmont, a land-locked region of Italy, seafood is still served though it comes mostly from the region to the south, Liguria. In fact, the two regions have developed a vibrant exchange business, trading the wine and grain from the north for the olives and seafood from the south. In this way, Piedmont is able to deliver a broad array of food all prepared by talented chefs.

The tablemates took advantage of this largesse. Beginning with *soma d'ai*, thick slices of bread rubbed with garlic, olive oil, and salt, they proceeded to fuller dishes of meat, seafood, and pasta. Rita recalled having *tinche all'agro* at Enzo's before, a fish that is floured and sautéed then topped with a sauce of vinegar, lemon, and sage. Stefano wanted beef, so he selected *brasato al Barolo*, with a side of the area's famous polenta.

Nicki ordered *fricandeau astigiano*, another dish of beef with a sauce of garlic, rosemary, onions, sage, and white wine. Francesco and Paolo decided on *gnocchi alla bava*, while Tomaso and ordered a fresh fish specialty of the day.

The waiter returned to the bar, handed the order to that man who stood polishing glasses, and circled the dining room to reach another table ready to place an order.

"But wait," interjected Paolo, addressing Riccardo. "You said there's no problem. And I'm sure that finding no virus is good. But there is still the problem of the missing truffles. Are you confident that we can eliminate virus from our list of possible reasons for the failed harvest?"

"Si, my young man," he replied. Then, with a broad smile and a wave of his glass toward the table, Riccardo added, "I vote for government conspiracy!"

There was little amusement shown for his jocular attitude, since most of the people at the table still showed concern about the present – and future – of truffles in Alba.

"Alright," said Tomaso, "we're down to theft or government conspiracy," but he said this last with less enthusiasm than the mycologist showed.

"There's as good a chance that global warming is to blame," said Francesco. The thought was ridiculous, and he meant it in rueful jest, but Nicki wasn't amused.

They talked about these possibilities as their dishes arrived, but all quickly came to the conclusion that, if global warming and government conspiracy were just ridiculous myths, then theft was the only likely cause.

"But who could do that," Tomaso nearly boomed. "Who would do that?" he added for emphasis.

So they were stuck. Slowly coming to the realization that the *tartufi* had been stolen right from the ground, the conversation flagged.

"*Per favore*," Stefano said, waving his fork in the direction of the *cameriere*. "Please bring a bottle, no, two bottles of Conterno Fantino Barolo," nodding his fork for emphasis, he added, "the Sorì Ginestra."

"*D'accordo*," said the waiter, offering his first smile of the evening. He seemed to like large parties, especially those who ordered expensive wines.

48

CATCHING UP

*H*e knew Lidia had help with the truck. She would need it because she couldn't drive both car and truck at once. And he knew where she would stash the truck, just where he had stashed the other car several days ago, so this time he didn't have to follow her to catch up.

He waited till the right hour then got in his car and drove north toward the French border, back to Modane where all this had begun. The truck could take care of itself; he wanted to see Lidia before she disappeared into the French countryside. At this late hour, he knew she'd spend one more night before moving on. She had her habits, too, although she thought he didn't know.

He also knew that she would, truly, disappear with everything they'd worked to achieve. He had learned from her; just as she *didn't trust anyone, he knew he couldn't trust her. So he assumed Lidia would take everything and leave him.*

"That is, if she didn't kill me first," he thought.

She didn't like loose ends. Otherwise, why did she insist that he kill the hunter? He was just teaching me, but that came too close to disclosure for her. He understood killing the fishermen a bit better, although those guys probably would have just disappeared back into their world and been no threat to them.

It was obvious she had to kill Alfonso. She had stolen his computer program allowing us to find all the truffle fields, and he would soon realize this. She would consider his death to be unavoidable.

The only one who knew more about her than Alfonso was her partner. The way he saw it, one more death was also unavoidable.

He pulled his car to the curb outside the hotel in Modane. It was already ten o'clock and many of the restaurants were closing. Just like in Italy, the cities in France stayed up late and people ate evening meals lasting close to midnight but, also just like in Italy, the rural areas turned down much earlier. Lidia would already have eaten her dinner. She would be in her room.

A bribe for the hotel clerk and a smile was all it took to convince him that the man was the guest's fiancé, long on the road and anxious to see his lover upstairs. He gave the visitor a key to the room without much effort.

The man climbed the stairs quietly and walked down the carpeted hallway with broad, soft steps. At Lidia's door he paused and considered the lock. He would have to turn it and open the door without a sound. Lidia would have a weapon by her bed and he did not want to risk a showdown. He wanted to win this battle without a struggle.

The lock yielded easily and the doorknob turned without a squeak. There was a sliver of light coming from the left as the man slowly swung the door open, just enough for him to step through.

Lidia stood less than ten feet from him, her back turned as she studied something on the desk by the window. He took two tentative steps toward her, reaching a spot just an arm's length away.

"Hello, Lidia," he said. Although he had surprised her, she did not startle. She just turned my way and stopped.

"Hello, Ruger," she said. "I didn't expect you tonight."

The few seconds that passed seemed like an hour. We exchanged glances, and her stare went from his face to his right hand.

"What's that?" she asked, catching the glimmer of the metal pick in my hand.

"Oh, it's a zappino," he said. "A truffle pick," he added, as he rolled the weapon back and forth between his fingers.

"I see." With that she brought her gaze back up to his face and he once again saw that black, empty look she gets sometimes, when she is at her scariest.

49

LA PASSEGGIATA

After the meal at dell'Enzo's, the entire group walked out the door and into a traditional Italian scene: the evening passeggiata was on full display. Riccardo excused himself to return home.

"Students may stay out late at night dreaming up difficult questions to ask *il professore*," he said. "But *il professore* cannot stay out late at night if he intends to answer all those questions!" With a tip of his hat, and a kiss for Rita and Nicki's hands, he turned about and headed down an avenue of sidewalk cafés.

"We have no choice," said Stefano with resignation. He wasn't referring to their actions, but to the realization that the *tartufi* were most likely stolen.

They walked on in silence for a while, separating into couples, with Tomaso and Paolo taking up the rear. Suddenly, a man stepped out from a darkened doorway and approached them.

"Are you the ones inquiring about the truffle harvest?" he asked, addressing Tomaso and Paolo.

The others were a couple of steps ahead but overheard the question and stopped to listen.

"Of course we're asking," began Tomaso, "but so is everyone."

Then, shrugging his shoulders, Tomaso asked the man what he knew.

"There are three rumors," he began, but was interrupted by Francesco who had returned to join them.

"Yes, there are three rumors, virus, government plot, and thievery." Francesco omitted global warming, but Paolo almost chimed in out of sheer absurdity.

"But, no," the stranger remarked. "Two of the rumors are for fools. No virus could occur that suddenly, and that widespread, without some forewarning. And the government, well those people might mess up our lives and our finances, but they wouldn't dare to mess up our food!"

By then, everyone in the group had collected around the stranger. Since he understood what they already knew, he must have accepted the premise that thieves were to blame. So what did he know that might help them?

"I was in my truffle field a few nights ago and I heard rustling among the trees," he began his story.

"Where?" asked Paolo, then he immediately realized that such a question is never asked of a *trifolào*.

The stranger looked at him dismissively, then continued.

"I thought it was a wild animal, maybe a truffle dog that had escaped his owner, so I approached carefully. Suddenly, there was a light, bright but not big, and then it went out."

"Was it a camera flash?" asked Nicki.

"No, longer than that, but not a flashlight because the light didn't have a beam. It just glowed, then went out. So I ran toward the trees because they were mine. Well, the truffle field was mine anyway. And I heard the rustling again. As I approached, my feet made sounds as I ran through the dry leaves, so the rustling stopped for a second, then it too ran off."

Knowing Italians' superstitious nature, Rita laughingly asked if it was a forest sprite.

"Of course not," the stranger replied with some irritation. "I know sprites. I've seen them before, and this was not one!"

"What do you think it was?" asked Tomaso.

"Just as the rustling sound was escaping me, and I followed its sound to track its direction, whatever made the sound approached the edge of the woods. There was only a little moonlight, but there was enough that I saw a man, hunched over, but it was clearly a man." And then to Rita, he repeated, "Not a sprite."

"Did you go to your field?" asked Stefano.

"Si, but it was dark and I didn't have my dogs with me. I didn't plan to hunt that night. Too bad, because they would have bitten his leg off."

"Was there enough light to see anything?" Stefano persisted.

"With my hands, I could tell that the ground was disturbed. I never leave it like that. Any respectable *trifolào* knows he has to smooth the ground after harvesting, or otherwise people will come by in daylight and see where the harvest took place. Then our secret will get out."

Paolo was enjoying adding this new chapter to his repertoire of truffle knowledge.

"When you harvest the truffle, you smooth the dirt. But all this takes place at night, in the dark," Paolo stated, as the stranger nodded assent.

"So, you are able to smooth the dirt so well, in the dark, that someone walking by in the daylight can't tell you've been there?" Paolo asked.

"Si. To be a *trifolào*, you must know many things, including how to cover up your tracks. Or else, you will own the truffle field for only one year!" Then, looking aside, he admitted that sometimes he uses the faint glow of his cell phone to check his work.

There was little more he could offer in terms of details or identity, so the group thanked him for his insights and wandered off.

They chose a table at the nearby café and their conversation wound through many topics, all except for truffles, which each and every person was relieved to avoid for a time. When Nicki turned to ask Paolo a question, she realized that he wasn't even beside her anymore. She looked toward the café where she discovered Paolo talking to a leggy brunette with deliciously red lipstick and a curvaceous body.

50

PRIMA COLAZIONE

Through the years, Rita and Stefano had returned to Alba, taking three days off on two consecutive weeks, to find the best truffle deals and bring the precious fungus back to Ristorante Girasole. It was a much-anticipated holiday, one that allowed them to blend business with the pleasure of visiting Alba, one of Italy's truly convivial old cities.

This year, they returned to find little to bring back and, although they tried to enjoy revisiting familiar restaurants and cafés, the disappointment with the truffle harvest laid heavily on their hearts.

The morning after their return to Alba, Rita and Stefano's thoughts were on each other. Restaurant owners worked long hours, and usually late into the night, so it would seem logical that most would sleep late into the morning. But most seasoned chefs and restaurateurs also knew that they had little time to themselves, which made dewy mornings in friendly cities a welcome mini-holiday. Rita and Stefano felt just this way, settling into chairs at their table at Caffé Revello.

Their talk centered on the menu at Ristorante Girasole, and they avoided as much as possible the topic of truffle dishes, which would be difficult to sustain this year. They talked about other menu items, focusing on the staple of Genoa, seafood.

"I think we should offer a few more options with beef and veal," said Stefano. He knew his wife's talents could easily include this, and he wanted their dining room to be celebrated for her unique style of cooking.

Rita sipped her cappuccino and listened to her husband's comments, but she could tell he was just trying to distract her from the specific problem with the truffles. She occasionally looked directly at Stefano, found a few moments of attention to give him, and followed his train of thought.

"Yes, I see," she replied, jotting thoughts down on a napkin. "Perhaps I can make up some recipes that include pasta in the preparation, more than just adding it as a side dish," she continued, still doodling. And then, just as quickly, her attention would veer elsewhere and she would be ruminating on matters to do with tubers, dogs, and oak trees - - and thieves.

"Ah, I know," Stefano broke in, "How about...," and they continued in this way for some time while drinking coffee and nibbling at the biscuits in the bowl on the table.

It was inevitable that the taboo subject would have to be raised.

Looking up at her husband with sadness in her eyes, Rita said, "But what about the *tartufi*?" as she laid the pen down on the table. It was a gesture full of meaning, as if today's market would give her nothing to jot down on her list of new menu possibilities.

Caffé Revello that morning was lightly traveled, with people coming in for a short cup of espresso and then wandering back out again as quickly as they came. Tourists were more in evidence since this place was on Piazza Cagnasso and the visitors to Alba had just discovered it two days earlier during the Palio, and now continued to return. Locals liked Caffé Revello exactly because it was out of the way, not on one of the main piazze like Risorgimento or Savona, but these same citizens of Alba knew they would have to share the tables with tourists for a brief time each year around the Palio.

Stefano looked at Rita, then away, past her shoulder and into the street beyond. He would regret not having the truffles, too. Maybe not as much as his culinary wife, but as a restaurant owner. When he glanced back at Rita, she was still looking at him, waiting for his answer.

"*Non so,*" he said, "I don't know," and their conversation died. It was as if touching the taboo subject had killed their fun.

51

CONFESSIONS

Paolo didn't follow the early morning routine of his aunt and uncle. As usual, he slept into the mid-morning hours, and Rita sent Nicki to bang on his door.

"Wake up, sleepy head," she called through the door. Hearing two voices through the wood, she stepped back expecting to be surprised. Surely not the brunette from last night, she thought.

Paolo pulled the door slightly ajar and greeted Nicki with a sheepish grin. Of course, she couldn't let him escape without full disclosure, so she had no qualms about pushing him gently to the side to see who his new friend was. Nicki's face brightened when she saw who was sitting on the bed brushing her hair.

"Lucia! So nice to see you here," Nicki added with a friendly chuckle, recalling the young lady from the café the previous weekend who shared a bottle of Moscato with Paolo.

Paolo knew that Nicki would just push her way in and take up too much space in his romantic little nest, so he gently nudged her back from the door, smiling and thanking her for waking him, and quietly pressed the door closed in Nicki's grinning face.

From behind the door, Nicki reminded him of the plans to have lunch together at Vincafé.

"Lucia is welcome, too," she chatted conspicuously through the closed door, knowing that this would force Paolo to bring her and face the chiding of the table for doing so.

Nicki skipped away with newfound pleasure and a great story to lead into the day.

Rita and Stefano were waiting on the terrazza of La Locanda Cortiletto d'Alba just before noon, reading the morning newspaper and waiting for their friends to join them. Nicki came first, and could barely contain her glee. She was bursting to tell them that the table would have to be set for one more, but when she was about to blurt it out, she saw Rita's eyes go wide.

Nicki threw a glance over her shoulder and saw Paolo and Lucia descending the steps together. Turning back around, she saw approving looks from Stefano and a somewhat more reserved, motherly approval from Rita. Spinning back once more, she greeted Paolo and Lucia warmly, and everyone was fully aware that Nicki would have some fun with this all day.

"Rita, Stefano," Nicki began, linking arms with Paolo's partner, "This is Lucia. We met her last week at the café. Remember?"

"Si, I remember," said Stefano, perhaps a bit too cheerfully, as Rita elbowed him in the ribs and shot him a stern look.

"*Buon giorno*," said Lucia, acting a bit shy knowing that she was the object of all this attention. She was as pretty at Nicki, but not as bold, so she looped her arm through Paolo's for support.

Paolo, too, showed a bit of shyness in this setting. He was self-assured in most things, but this awkward meeting in the hotel lobby seemed too much like bringing the girlfriend home to meet the family.

An uncomfortable moment passed, and it was Nicki who got them back on track. She wanted to make amends for embarrassing Lucia, so she stole her from Paolo and walked toward the door, telling her new female friend all about their adventures in Alba to date. Lucia was already more informed than Nicki realized, but she kept her silence and let Nicki continue.

The rest followed them out the door and, as Stefano whispered his compliments to Paolo, Rita cuffed her husband in the head.

Tomaso and Francesco were already seated in Vincafé when they arrived. The midday crowd was beginning to gather and Tomaso knew to arrive early and secure a table in the corner of the cantina below ground, or else the party would be dispossessed and have to find another place for their lunch.

A brief version of the morning surprise introductions was repeated here. Tomaso showed Paolo his unsuppressed approval, without letting on that he already knew Lucia and her father from the truffle business. "Paolo's found a very smart woman," Tomaso thought to himself. .

"*Cameriere,*" called Tomaso, "a bottle of Attilio Ghisolfi Barbera and one of Bongiovanni Arneis, *per favore.*"

That they would talk about truffles was undeniable; that they would wait till the meal had begun was the challenge. Many of the comments excluded background from their earlier conversations, since all at the table knew each other and the situation well. Paolo fed Lucia additional details about what the group had been doing, pointing out that Rita and Stefano owned a restaurant in Genoa, that they made annual visits to Alba to buy truffles for their menu, and that Tomaso was a *trifolào* of great standing in the city.

"*Si, io so*," she said, "I know." Tomaso grinned at the acknowledgement, and Paolo looked at him a bit miffed and confused.

"Lucia's father is a fine truffle hunter," Tomaso pointed out, nodding his recognition in Lucia's direction. She smiled.

"His field is not far from mine," Tomaso added.

Somehow this news both settled Paolo and unsettled him. He knew that he was with someone who understood the culture and traditions of truffles, but he also realized that his new education would probably be insignificant next to Lucia's.

" Then you're familiar with the rumors of the truffle harvest," Stefano said to Lucia.

"Si," she said, and raised her eyebrows in mild horror. "Si, I know," she sighed, "and my father is devastated. Fortunately, our family income had not been devastated."

Tomaso explained to everyone that Lucia's father was an engineer who hunted truffles simply because his family had always done so.

"The traditions of the *trifolài* must remain unbroken," he added, and Lucia nodded her agreement. Her brother would no doubt take up the tradition for her family; girls seldom became *trifolài*.

With each new revelation about Lucia's background, Paolo became more impressed. As he sat back to reevaluate her, Lucia glanced his way with a kind, yet slightly proud, smile stitched across her face.

While they ate, Tomaso opened the discussion of truffles. He pressed the point about thieves, and they all talked about how one person – or team – could pull this off.

"How would they know where the fields are?" Tomaso repeated. Stefano offered the opinion that truffle fields are revisited each year, so how can they remain secret forever. Tomaso reminded him that even subtle shifting of the location, something that is necessary every year, would throw off the thieves even if they knew last year's locations.

"Besides, there is honor among *trifolài*," he added. "We would not disturb each others' fields. Even the Albese who do not hunt for truffles would leave our fields alone."

"Possibly," Paolo suggested, "the thieves have abducted the truffle hunters' dogs while the *trifolài* are gone during the day. These *cani da tartufo* would lead them right to the truffle grounds."

Tomaso approved of Paolo's theory, but pointed out the error in his reasoning was an error of culture and tradition.

"A truffle hunter's dogs would only work for him and they would not listen to someone else. Besides, most truffle hunters work at home, in their fields, during the day." With a nod to Lucia, he added, "Some *trifolài* are highly educated, like Lucia's father, and they work elsewhere, but most of us would know if our dogs had gone missing during the day."

Throughout the conversation, both Stefano and Tomaso noticed that Francesco remained very quiet. He was experienced and knowledgeable on the subject, and was not usually reluctant to throw his opinion into the debate. But he was silent today.

"Francesco, *che é la problema?*" his father queried, "what's the problem?"

Francesco didn't immediately respond and Nicki cast a dark look in his direction.

"Hey, Francesco, your father is asking you a question," she prodded.

Francesco looked around the table and took a long gulp from the glass of wine before him. He began to respond, but did so looking down at the plate of food that remained largely untouched.

"Alfonso," was all he could say at first.

The table grew silent and everyone looked at him.

"*Che é cosa?*" his father asked. "What is it?"

"Alfonso and I were drinking one night," Francesco began his story feebly, "and he said he could write a program to find all the truffle fields."

"That's ridiculous. What program?" Tomaso asked, his face beginning to take on a reddish hue.

"It uses GPS. In cell phones," Francesco admitted. "It could track cell phones as they move around."

"And...?" prodded Lucia.

"So he bet that he could find all the truffle fields by plugging in cell numbers from the *trifolài*... which I supplied him." Francesco was staring down at his plate, his hands folded meekly on his lap.

"What!" his father burst out. "Why did you do that?"

"It was just a game," Francesco said, to shaking heads all around. "We weren't going to do anything with it. But someone must have gotten his program...and the cell numbers I gave him."

Tomaso stood up, started toward the steps out of the cantina, turned back, and sat down again. His energy was rising and he didn't know how to defuse it.

"*Serpente!*" he spat out.

Francesco explained that Alfonso boasted of inventing a way to find each truffle field. Francesco said he didn't believe him and Alfonso wanted to prove how smart he was. They were out drinking late at night and Alfonso's claim sounded like nothing but a manly boast. They made a bet, shook hands on it, and laughed about it afterwards.

But a few days later, Francesco and Alfonso realized that truffles began disappearing and they were scared that someone had stolen the program.

"We've got to do something," Francesco reported telling Alfonso. "People depend on these for their livelihood."

As far as Tomaso was concerned, this was no game. His own son, and that shiftless failed farmer that he called a friend, had set in motion a terrible theft of the region's most cherished treasure.

"Get up," Tomaso demanded, standing and signaling to the waiter.

"You're going to take us to Alfonso right now, and we're going to settle this thing up with him." Tomaso's words carried such anger that the "settling" could well include stringing Alfonso up from the bell tower.

Vincafe's owner happened by and Tomaso explained that they would be leaving the meal early, to hold the check for him and they would return later.

"*Si, d'accordo*," said the restaurateur, surprised that an entire table would depart without finishing the meal. Tomaso assured him that it had nothing to do with the food, and that they would surely return.

With that, Tomaso grabbed Francesco by the shirt and dragged him out of the dining room and up the steps into the daylight, trailing a menacing silence behind them.

52

DARK SECRETS

Tomaso was so ashamed of his son's involvement in the truffle theft that he didn't want the rest of them to follow. Standing on the sidewalk outside the Vincafé, he tried to calm himself and explain to Rita and Stefano why they should stay behind. He put up his hand in a strained, but non-menacing gesture, to indicate that he didn't want to be followed.

To Lucia, Tomaso's words took on an apologetic tone, since he knew that her family was more directly affected by his son's actions. To Paolo and Nicki, he simply asked for their patience.

"I'm going too," declared Nicki.

"*No, mi'amore,*" Tomaso replied with fatherly kindness. "I cannot let you do that. This is for me – and Francesco – to fix."

They walked off toward the car that Francesco had parked around the corner, leaving the others to just stand and wonder how this would play out.

Francesco leaned back into the driver's seat, and nervously watched his father slide into the seat beside him. The heat from Tomaso's anger permeated the small confines of the car, and Francesco knew that this would only get worse.

"Where is he?" is all Tomaso had to say.

"I don't know; I haven't seen him today and he isn't answering his phone. We can try his apartment, but he also has a warehouse outside of Alba."

Tomaso looked at his son, almost surprised by his level of incompetence at this moment.

"And, if he's part of this grand theft, don't you think he'd use his warehouse to hide them?"

"Papa, Alfonso isn't the thief," but Francesco knew his father wouldn't automatically buy into that excuse, so he set the car in gear and headed out of town.

They drove out of Alba to the refrigerated warehouse that Alfonso used to store the fruit that he sells to the markets and restaurants in the area. Francesco knew the area well, and also knew Alfonso's business; they had been friends for years. In fact, Francesco recalled a younger, introverted Alfonso who liked to tinker with computer programs and was not much of a farmer. Francesco wondered why his friend agreed to enter the family business instead of working in some office in Turin or Milan.

Throughout the ride, Tomaso remained resolutely quiet. It was probably better for both men, since words would come out in an explosion, and little positive would be accomplished.

Francesco pulled the car to a stop in front of the warehouse and they approached the broad double doors to the building. They were closed, but not locked, so the two men grabbed the handles and swung the doors open. Inside, the first room was small and furnished with a desk, a couple of chairs and some filing cabinets. A small laptop computer sat on the desk, its screen saver displaying alternating images of the Italian countryside. There were no sounds except for the pulsating rhythm of the cooling unit that maintained the refrigerator temperatures of the back room. A few lights were on, and the room seemed like it had been used very recently.

Familiar with the layout of the warehouse, Francesco strode across the office and pushed open the long, heavy rubber mats that hung across the doorway and separated the office from the chilled storage area. That room was dark, but Francesco knew where the light switch was. He turned to his right, reached across the flaps of the doorway to the metal-sheathed wall of this huge refrigeration room, and flipped the switch up.

The lights came on just as Tomaso stepped between the flaps. Both men looked at the room, which had some boxes of produce stacked around its perimeter. In the corner of the room was a chair, with Alfonso gagged and tied to it.

Francesco was startled by the sight and rushed to his friend to release him. But as he drew close to Alfonso, Francesco let out a whimper of shock and fear. Seeing the streak of red that ran from Alfonso's temple down to his reddened collar, Francesco knew he had come too late.

"*Mama santa!*" Tomaso's shout echoed off the metallic walls of the room.

Both men approached Alfonso's unmoving body, examined the wound to the temple, and knew that it had been created by a gunshot.

"What is this?" Tomaso screamed. Realizing that his son was somehow involved in truffle theft and, now, murder, left him with nothing but curses to hurl at the room.

Francesco was shell-shocked and stood stock still in panic. His mind retraced all the things that had happened, and all the things that he and Alfonso had talked about, but he couldn't put his finger on what trail led to this ending.

Where was Lidia? Francesco immediately suspected Alfonso's girlfriend and looked around the room for evidence that she had been there. Finding none, he returned to Alfonso's lifeless body and searched for clues.

Again he found nothing. In fact, he found nothing at all. Alfonso's wallet, keys, gold ring, and cell phone were missing. Was this just a botched robbery? Had someone barged in on Alfonso, then killed him in a rage? That would have been more reassuring, in a sick way, but Francesco knew that this had more to do with the truffles than that. Otherwise, why would he be tied to a chair.

"Is this where the truffles were kept?" Tomaso asked.

"I told you, Alfonso didn't steal the truffles," although Francesco was now beginning to doubt this.

"Humph," Tomaso replied in disgust. "Was Alfonso killed for the truffles?"

"He would not have struggled, with anyone. Alfonso was a coward," Francesco had to admit. "If there were truffles here, he would have invited the thieves to take them as long as they left him alone."

This didn't solve the mystery, but Tomaso also realized that they could no longer avoid the police.

"What could be so important about truffles, that they would kill my friend?" Francesco pleaded.

"You had better be more selective of friends in the future, my son. Now, we must return to Alba and notify the police."

53

A SOMBER DRIVE

F rancesco and Tomaso returned to the car, lowered themselves into the seats while still distracted by their find, and they spent a slow, quiet drive back to Alba. Francesco's hands gripped the wheel with a fierceness borne of regret and suspicion. He couldn't stop thinking about Lidia, hating her, somehow knowing that she must be the cause of all this. He resolved to find her as soon as he made his way back to Alba.

Pulling the car to a stop beside the piazza, Francesco and Tomaso quickly leaped out.

"I'm going to find Lidia," Francesco declared.

"No, you're not. We're going to the police and report this. And I hope your involvement is no more than the theft of the great jewel of the Piedmont!"

After making a full report to the police, father and son were dismissed and allowed to return to their other responsibilities. The police planned a trip to Alfonso's warehouse, but they didn't want a civilian along for the ride.

"We don't need any help there," Captain Mussino told them, and added sternly, "but if there is no body, I will not be pleased."

Francesco pondered the slightly morbid way the captain wished to find a dead body, but he also knew that if something untoward became of Alfonso's remains, this matter would become even more complicated.

Tomaso called Rita and asked her to gather everyone to meet in Piazza Risorgimento to explain what had happened. Moments later, they were all there, including Lucia, since she craved information on this no less than the others.

"He'll explain," barked Tomaso, with a thumb jerked in Francesco's direction, punctuating the statement with a piercing glare.

"Alfonso is dead," he blurted out. It seemed easier to tell the story once that point was made.

Francesco retreated to the beginning of the story, explaining that he and Alfonso had argued, in a friendly way, about the great secrecy that surrounded truffle hunting. How every *trifolào* maintained his own fields and was absolutely certain that no one could discern where he hunted. The darkness of night was some cover, although the rustling of dogs on the stillness of night likely gave away even the most discrete of *trifolài*, but the mystique was maintained.

Alfonso bet Francesco that he could weasel the information out of the *trifolài* and they would reveal their hunting grounds to him. Francesco scoffed at the idea.

"No hunter would give up that information," said Lucia, and her words made it clear that she was blaming Francesco and Alfonso for all of this.

"That would violate hundreds of years of tradition," Stefano said, "and jeopardize their own harvest."

Francesco continued with his story, explaining that Alfonso persisted in his boast. At first, he told Francesco that he just planned to write this program to prove he could do it.

"But he was not a truffle hunter," Francesco explained, as if anyone needed to hear that. "And he didn't know all of them.

"He knew I was a *trifolào*," and here he paused under the accusatory glare of his father, "and so he asked me for all the hunters' names and cell phone numbers so he could contact them.

"We were drinking and, under the influence of wine, I still considered Alfonso's boast an empty threat. So I checked his own cell phone and, with the help of pen and paper from the bar, I began to write down cell numbers for all the *trifolài* that I know in the city."

"Why did you give him that?" Tomaso boomed. "He's untrustworthy!"

Francesco explained that Alfonso was his friend and, besides, this was just a game.

"It's not a game!" Tomaso shouted.

Later, according to Francesco, Alfonso proudly showed him a computer program he had written. It used cell numbers and GPS information to track the movements of everyone holding those phones.

Francesco continued, "Unfolding the lid of his laptop, he showed me a map that was displayed on the screen, with dozens of circled letters. Some of these letters were moving; some were still. The map was Alba and the surrounding area and the letters corresponded to a legend at the bottom of the screen."

Francesco told them that he read the legend and immediately recognized the names of the *trifolài* that he had given to Alfonso. He looked back at the moving figures on the screen and immediately realized what Alfonso had done.

Lucia demanded to know if Francesco had given Alfonso her father's cell number. Francesco looked at her as if he was about to lie, but her glare froze him. He looked down at his feet and returned to his story.

"It takes a few minutes for a trained *cano da tartufo* to find the truffle and for the hunter to unearth it," Francesco said, and "Alfonso knew that any such delays would indicate that the *trifolào* had found truffles at that exact spot, a spot that his program could record."

Francesco clearly didn't want to go on, but Lucia picked up the thread of the description.

"Yes, a recording of all the places where the *trifolài* found their truffles, a recording that could help a thief steal these treasures right from under our noses!" Lucia's use of "our," combined with her raised fist, was as menacing as it was climactic.

Francesco told everyone that he objected to this program, and had told Alfonso to destroy it. But Alfonso was too proud of his computing achievement, yet he promised not to tell anyone.

But, by now, everyone standing in this small group on this street in Alba knew that either Alfonso told, or someone else found out about his program.

"Italian men can't help but boast to their girlfriends," Nicki said. With that, she gave Francesco a withering look, one that made the young man shrink from her gaze. She's mad as hell, he thought to himself, and she doesn't look like she's going to calm down.

"So, now, where's Lidia?" Rita asked. It was a question that everyone wanted an answer to.

54

A THIEF IS NAMED

"How are you going to make this right?" asked Tomaso. "Truffles are not just a commodity or an ingredient in everyday dishes. They are the jewels of the Piedmont, prized throughout the world. And you have helped a thief with no honor to take our treasure, sell it, and ruin our hunting grounds. What will happen next?" he cried.

"We didn't help them steal the truffles," Francesco said.

"Yes, you did," Tomaso barked in anger.

"Well, I didn't mean to. And I certainly didn't have anything to do with Alfonso's murder."

They exchanged heated theories on the whereabouts of the missing truffles, the identity of the murderer, and what steps to take next. Most of the attention was on Lidia since none of them had seen her since the day before. But she was not from Alba and didn't even seem that interested in the culinary feats of the *tartufo*.

"But she would be interested in the commercial feats of it," declared Stefano.

Captain Mussino appeared at the edge of the group and approached Tomaso.

"My men have been to the warehouse. It is as you reported, a dead body, probably of a gunshot wound to the left temple, and that's all," he reported. Francesco was surprised that he found himself relieved by the news, but his friend was already dead; he didn't want the police to drive out there and find nothing.

"Any evidence of why it happened?" Tomaso asked. He had omitted reference to Alfonso's involvement in the grand theft of truffles in his earlier report, and once again decided to keep that out of the conversation. There was nothing specifically illegal about the truffle trade, but most of the sales took place outside of normal commerce and so no tax was being paid on them. The police even preferred to look the other way – occasionally rewarded for their oblivious stance with a handful of the blessed tubers – but the *fisco,* the tax man would be more curious about the trade. Tomaso was not only saving the *trifolài* by not mentioning the part played by truffles in this murder investigation, he was actually saving the police from a lot of unnecessary, and unwanted, work to cover up the theft.

"No evidence yet. We found many fingerprints around the facility, but they will not help much. It was frequented by Alfonso's workers, the local market men, restaurant owners, and many others." Mussino seemed already exhausted just listing the possible suspects. "We'll give this some thought and you'll probably hear from us later."

He turned to leave and made it just a few steps before pausing and turning around.

"One thing, though. A farmer who works near the warehouse reported seeing a strange truck approach the building, remain for about an hour, and then leave. It's probably nothing, but we'll be looking into that also."

55

TAMPERING WITH THE EVIDENCE

Before Captain Mussino was able to escape the group, Francesco had a brainstorm, and called after him.

"*Capitano! Aspetta, per favore*," he called out, "wait, please."

"Your men inspected the office and the refrigerated room, si?"

"Yes, they did."

"And they saw the things that Alfonso had there."

"Uh, yes, but what is your concern?" Mussino asked, a bit confused by the line of questioning.

"Let's see, Alfonso had his office, his filing cabinets, which I'm sure were filled with possibly useful information, and his laptop."

"Si," Mussino said, drawing out the single syllable as if to draw out a better explanation from Francesco.

"Did your men secure any of that information, for example, the files in the file cabinet?"

"No, not yet, they want the forensics team to go there first, and they won't be ready until after they've had their dinner." It was a time-weary story about Italian police. They were well intentioned, and the upper ranks were serious policemen, but the rank and file behind the badge seldom let duty interfere with the customs of their homeland, and one of the most cherished customs was eating.

"Grazie," said Francesco, and to make a finer point, "Then all the things are still there?"

"Yes, as I said," repeated Mussino, who then cast a suspicious eye on Francesco.

Francesco only smiled and replied, "Good, good," and nearly skipped away back to his father and the others gathered there.

"What was that about?" his father asked.

"Alfonso's laptop is still at the warehouse," Francesco reported.

"Of course," Tomaso said, "and that's where it's going to stay."

"But no," Francesco disagreed. "We need that computer. Alfonso taught me to use his program."

Confused looks from everyone circled Francesco, so he continued.

"Father, remember, we thought Alfonso had been robbed, his wallet, ring, and keys were gone...and so was his cell phone."

As if it was still not clear enough, Francesco triumphantly proclaimed that he might be able to find the thief by using Alfonso's program to trace the movements of his own phone!

Tomaso considered this, but Paolo interrupted their thoughts.

"Mussino made it clear that his forensics team was coming by later today. I think they'll know if the laptop has been taken."

Francesco smiled again. "Don't worry. Alfonso and I bought our laptops the same day, at the same store. In fact, we have the same model, if you understand what I mean."

"You're going to swap your laptop for his?" Nicki asked..
"Of course. So the police will have their laptop and we'll have Alfonso's program."

"Great, wonderful," said an exasperated Tomaso, raising his palms in near surrender. "You may escape involvement in the murder, so let's tamper with the evidence, just for fun!"

"It's definitely not for fun," was Francesco's quick retort. "But it may be the only way we can find the truffles and, if you care, Alfonso's killer."

"Let's go," said Paolo, recognizing that time was against them. It was already seven o'clock in the evening. The police would probably eat early just so they could get to the warehouse before it was too late.

"I'll drive," said Francesco, but Tomaso stopped him.

"Your car is too small. We'll take my fruit truck. At least you and I can fit in the front seat, and Paolo and Stefano can ride in back."

"What about us?" complained Nicki, referring to herself and Rita and Lucia.

"Alfonso's body is still there," said Francesco, "do you really want to see that?"

The women looked at each other, perhaps waiting for a volunteer and, seeing none, Nicki just waved the men away.

56

TWISTING THE FACTS

Tomaso made a detour going out of town to run by their house. Coming to a quick stop in front, Francesco jumped out and returned almost immediately with his laptop. Before they could leave, Dolce, Tomaso's best truffle dog, leaped into the back of the truck. It took Tomaso only seconds to conclude that the dog would refuse to get out, and he might come in handy looking for the pilfered truffles.

Tomaso was about to speed off when Francesco called out, "Stop."

"What? What's the matter?" Tomaso said.

"I need one thing more," Francesco said before running back into the house and returning moments later.

He had a small thumb drive in his hand and waved it at his father as if he expected a congratulatory slap on the back. Tomaso didn't even understand computers, so this tiny little instrument meant nothing to him.

"If I'm going to leave my laptop there," Francesco explained, "I want to make copies of my files on here," as he indicated the thumb drive, "then delete them all from the laptop. It would be better if the police found nothing on the computer they think is Alfonso's than if they found a bunch of files belonging to me."

"The polizia aren't stupid. They will be able to tell from the computer who the owner is," Tomaso said.

"Actually, no," Francesco replied, surprised that his father would know that much about computers. "Alfonso has friends in the computer business, and he gets a discount of purchases. He bought both computers in his own name and just gave this one to me."

Speeding down the rural roads to the warehouse, the men were more excited now than before. Stefano and Paolo discussed the chances of finding the truffles, and even Tomaso grudgingly spoke to his errant son about finding a solution to the mess.

When they pulled up to the warehouse, they saw a police car parked out front. All four men exchanged surprised glances, recalling Mussino's comment that the police were gone, and would return later. Of course, they would not have left a dead body unattended. There must be an officer inside, making sure no one tampered with the evidence. Which was exactly what they intended to do.

They knew the sound of their truck must have alerted the guard, so they conferred quickly about next steps.

"They don't know I found him there," offered Francesco, "so why not say that Captain Mussino, who knows I'm a friend of Alfonso, sent me here to identify the body. Remember, there was no identification left behind."

"Great, except for one thing," countered Paolo. "Actually, two things. If you didn't find the body, how would you know there was no identification? And besides, all we need is for the policeman to pass that information on to the captain, and he'll come after us."

"And another thing," added Stefano. "We can't all go in there, and it makes sense for you, Francesco, to stay out in the office while we distract the policeman and you're switching laptops."

All good points he had to admit. Then Tomaso chimed in.

"So, we need Francesco to stay out in the office and only one, perhaps more, of us to go inside."

Nods all around.

"Okay," Tomaso continued. "We need to play as dumb as that man inside guarding the body. Follow me."

With a finger to his lips, Tomaso reminded Dolce to keep quiet, and the four men left the truck.

They drew the warehouse door open slowly, but deliberately. Seeing no one in the office, Tomaso silently motioned for Francesco to go over to the desk and begin the swapping operation. Then Tomaso signaled for Stefano and Paolo to follow him into the refrigerator room.

As they stepped through the flaps shutting the office out from the storage unit, a twenty-something policeman stood up from a folding chair in the corner. He put his hand on his sidearm, but suspended his motion when Tomaso raised his hands.

"*Signore, io sono Tomaso,*" he began, introducing himself. He proceeded to introduce his friends while still holding his hands in the air. Slowly, as he sensed the officer relaxing, he lowered his hands.

"Did Captain Mussino tell you we were coming?" he asked.

Before the policeman could answer, Stefano picked up on the ruse, and chimed in.

"No, Tomaso. Captain Mussino said the officer asked you to come, to identify the body."

"I didn't ask you to come," said the officer.

"I didn't say you asked," said Stefano, "I said Captain Mussino said you asked."

Paolo had caught on quickly too and joined in.

"No, no. Captain Mussino asked Alfonso's girlfriend to come to identify the body," and, turning to the officer, he asked, "Is she here yet?"

"Oh, yes, she asked us to meet her here," added Tomaso.

"No, I left her back at the hotel," said Paolo.

By then the three men were conferring with each other as if the officer was not even in the room. The policeman stood by, with growing confusion, while the visitors debated who was supposed to be where. A moment later,

Francesco walked in. This time, feeling outnumbered and ill at ease, the officer did draw his weapon.

All four men raised their hands and offered muted protests.

"Please, signore, don't shoot," pleaded Tomaso, but he was equally sure the officer was too uncertain of the situation to risk firing his weapon.

With Tomaso bowing backward toward the door, the others followed suit, never once lowering their hands, and repeating apologies for disturbing the policeman. When they worked their way back into the office, Tomaso looked at Francesco, who merely offered a nod of success, and the four walked out to the truck.

"He'll never report that to Mussino," said Tomaso confidently. "He's too confused to sort it out."

Paolo, whose love of baseball made him a fan of the legendary routine of comedians Abbott and Costello, "Who's on First," couldn't help but smile at how easy it was to wreak havoc with someone's ability to reason.

They boarded the truck and sped away, but went only a safe distance before Tomaso pulled onto the grassy shoulder to watch what Francesco was doing. Paolo and Stefano craned their necks from the back of the truck to watch also.

Francesco tapped the keyboard of Alfonso's laptop and the program sprang into action. He keyed in Alfonso's cell phone, crossing his fingers that the person who stole it had the phone on. GPS tracking could work without activating the phone, but that way was easier and faster.

After a few minutes, the results displayed on the screen. It was a small town west of Torino, called Bordanecchia, about one hour's drive from their current location.

"I'll take the A21 around Torino," said Tomaso, "then head west on A32."

"Sure, that tracks the location of the phone. I'll keep this tuned in so we can use the GPS to zero in on the phone," added Francesco.

"Aren't you forgetting something?" came Paolo's voice from the back of the truck.

Francesco and Tomaso looked at each other for the answer.

"He's right," injected Stefano. "There are three ladies back in Alba who won't be happy about being left out of this."

Tomaso wanted to object, that this was no adventure for women, but he knew Stefano was right. Francesco placed a quick call to Nicki and told them where to meet the men. Lucia offered her car since she was the only local, and the women quickly drove to the meeting point.

On their way through Alba before heading west, the men swung off the road and waved as they passed Lucia's car. It roared to life and screeched onto the roadway as Lucia showed that Italian women could handle a car just as well as the men.

"Hmmm," Stefano muttered from the back of the truck. And, looking at Paolo bumping along next to him on the metal flatbed, he added, "You've got a lot of woman to manage there!"

57

BORDANECCHIA

They made it to Bordanecchia in little over an hour, a distance covered faster than the advisable speeds on the internet. As Francesco zoomed in on the map to get better detail on the exact location of the phone, Tomaso slowed the truck and listened for instructions. Lucia backed off on her speed too, but seemed restless to cover more ground.

"Here," then Francesco paused, and pointed, "no, turn left," each word spoken with great concentration. They had departed the paved roads and were now winding down dirt trails that were only slightly rutted from automobile tires. The trees closed in on both sides of the truck and blocked the last rays of light from the setting sun. Everyone seemed to sense the same thing, that unless they found that phone soon, it would be too dark to finish this tonight. They also knew that the battery on Alfonso's phone might soon give out and they, too, would be left in the dark.

"*Piano, piano,*" Francesco said, "Slowly, slowly," holding up his left hand as if to signal his meaning to Tomaso.

Suddenly, Tomaso slammed on the brakes and Lucia nearly ran into the truck. Francesco had been staring at the computer screen on his lap and, with his head bowed, almost flew forward into the windshield. He looked first at his father, then ahead.

Tomaso's headlights illuminated a circle of trucks, tents, and wagons gathered in a clearing in the woods. There was a fire burning in the middle and a number of people standing or sitting around it. The unexpected approach of the truck and car drew these people's attention, a small crowd that didn't expect to be disturbed in their campsite.

The men stepped out of the truck and the women left their car to join them. The people around the fire remained at attention, but three broke free to see who their visitors were.

"They're Zingari," whispered Lucia. "Gypsies. There are a few tribes like this in northern Italy. I've heard of them but I never travel this far from the city, so I've never met any."

Zingari are members of a loose diaspora called Romani, gypsies who live outside the populated areas of many countries, mostly in Europe, and about whom many stories are told.

"Are they dangerous?" asked Paolo. He was intrigued but also a bit put off. There were no Zingari in Tuscany and this reminder brought on pangs of homesickness, as Paolo suddenly longed for the quiet agrarian life of Sinalunga.

"No, they're not dangerous," Lucia assured him. "But many dark stories are told of their lifestyle."

"None true," added Tomaso. He had spent a long life in northern Italy and, unlike young Lucia, Tomaso had had the opportunity to meet many Zingari in the past. Some he counted as decent folks, some even friends, although the Zingari never wanted to spend enough time around a city to actually maintain friendships with mainstream people.

Two men and a woman approached them. Without offering his hand, the first one spoke in guarded tones.

"Why have you come into our home?"

"We are looking for something," Tomaso said. As the oldest of the group, he felt it best to take charge.

"And what are you looking for?"

Tomaso introduced himself and the others. He briefly summarized the events of the last few days, leaving out the part about Alfonso's death. He correctly assumed that bringing the subject of murder into this conversation would shut down the exchange.

"So," said the Zingari, "you've come to find your truffles?" He and his companions laughed at the ridiculous comment.

"No," said Tomaso evenly. "We've come because we are looking for a friend's cell phone. Because it was taken from him and we believe that, where the cell phone is, the truffles might be found."

The Zingari looked at Tomaso with a more studied look.

"You think we stole something?" It was a charge often leveled at Zingari, people who were frequently blamed by civilians and government officials for anything they couldn't otherwise explain.

"No," Tomaso said, looking for the right words. "But maybe you found something," he added, never wavering in his eye contact with the Zingari.

Finally, the Zingari offered his hand.

"I am Pongo. This is Calvi," indicating the man next to him, "and she is Marita. We have stolen nothing, but we did find this," and he pulled Alfonso's cell phone from his pocket.

With that gesture, Dolce bounded up to the man and sniffed his hand. Zingari don't keep dogs but are not afraid of them either. So Pongo didn't flinch, but wondered what the dog was smelling.

"Could I see that?" asked Francesco, reaching for the phone. He took it from Pongo while Dolce continued his inspection. With a soft "ruff," and a nod of his head, Dolce communicated to Tomaso that he smelled truffles.

"What's he doing?" asked Marita about the dog's behavior.

Tomaso wanted to smile, but restrained himself. "He smells truffles. He is *un cano da tartufo*."

Pongo relaxed a bit and decided to speak openly. He said that he and his friends helped a woman move a truck that, apparently, was broken down on the crest of a hill not far from their camp. Yes, the truck might have been holding truffles, he admitted. She had come to them on Sunday, two days ago, said she needed to have her truck fixed and would they be able to do that. She offered 100 euros just to bring her truck down the mountain.

Calvi added that the woman was not from this region and they didn't think she had any friends in Alba or elsewhere in Piedmont. It was clear that she wanted their help because she didn't want anyone in the local towns to know her or what she was doing.

Marita said that the woman was not at all friendly, but the Zingari were ready to help her for a fee. She didn't have to explain, but Tomaso knew that these tribes made their living not by stealing from other Italians, but by earning money on the margins of society. Driving a truck a few hours would be a simple and incidental way of picking up some extra euros.

As they exchanged details, the Zingari said the woman told them where to meet her, deep in the woods off a main road in Piedmont. She was there at the appointed time, where Calvi and Marita quickly figured out that one of distributor wires on her truck had burned out. They replaced it with some wire they had in their own car, and Calvi took the wheel while Marita drove her car back down the mountain.

"Then," Marita continued, "the woman said since she had driven her own car to this place she couldn't drive both her car and the truck."

"Right," said Lucia, "she drove to the broken down truck to meet you. She had her own car.

"So I drove the truck," said Calvi, "and in tandem we drove around Alba, past Torino, and gathered up at Bordanecchia."

"We left the truck where she instructed and we climbed into Marita's car and returned to our camp."

The Zingari said they didn't know the woman's name.

"How is it you still have the phone?" asked Paolo.

"That was part of our fee," responded Pongo.

"And what about the truffles?" asked Lucia.

"Do we look like great chefs?" asked Marita. "What would we do with those?"

Pongo offered a bit more detail. "She asked how she could get back to A32, the highway that heads across the border into France."

Tomaso and the others looked at each other.

"She's taking the truffles into France?" It was more of a question than a statement from Paolo. It certainly seemed that way, but Tomaso was doubtful and laughed at the irony. The French have always boasted that their black Périgord truffles are superior to Alba's white truffle. So why smuggle Italy's finest into a land that is too smug to accept the *Tuber magnatum*?

Tomaso thanked Pongo and the others for their time, then waved for his companions to follow him back to the truck.

58

PASSING THE BORDER INTO FRANCE

"There are no truffles here. That's plain to see," Tomaso told them.

"But how do you know?" asked Paolo. "What about searching their trucks?"

Tomaso looked at his young apprentice with fading pride, but Lucia stepped in to rescue Paolo.

"Dolce is trained to find truffles. If there was a cache of *tartufi* at that campsite, he would have been over there in a second."

Paolo recognized his mistake, and nodded his head in acquiescence.

"Let's go," said Tomaso.

"Where?" asked Rita.

"We're going to follow the trail. Up A32 and then we'll let Dolce do the rest."

As they boarded their vehicles, Paolo wondered whether this dog could actually sniff out a truckload of truffles from a distance, but he decided to keep quiet rather than risk showing off his ignorance once again.

Bordanecchia is not far from the French border, and the town of Modane lay straight ahead. With the creation of the European Union and the later establishment of the Schengen treaty to manage customs between the countries, not every road had border controls. This was true of A32, which turned into France's N543 after the border, but not every road was totally outside of control. Everyone in the truck and following car knew that they might be challenged by French officials at any point.

Tomaso passed over the border and kept his vigilance up. Francesco, with no computer to monitor anymore, surveilled the countryside and tried to pick up signs that Lidia had passed through the area. Neither of them, nor the other men and women trailing behind, had any idea what to look for. Lidia could be hours ahead, or miles away, but they were hoping to get lucky.

Nightfall had come, but they continued on. Coming around a bend, Tomaso saw a lighted building up ahead on the left of the roadway. A uniformed man stepped into the light cast by a tall lamppost, and indicated for Tomaso to stop the truck.

Tomaso told the guard that they were tourists, an extended family from Alba, and they wanted to visit Modane for the night. It was late and he asked the guard for hotel suggestions.

The guard looked skeptical at first, and shone his flashlight into each of the vehicles. After a brief series of questions, he offered some hotel suggestions, admitting that he was a local and, therefore, not used to finding hotels in his home city.

"We might also want to find some of your famous truffles here," said Tomaso with a glint in his eye. He hoped this might pry some additional information out of the guard. Tomaso was estimating that this soldier would know little about truffles, and that he wouldn't even know that the Périgord truffles are harvested in spring, not fall. But the ploy was worth a try.

The guard flinched, just a bit, just enough to telegraph to Tomaso that there was more information to be had here.

"Have you seen anyone transporting truffles through here?" he asked directly.

The guard breathed deeply and looked away.

"Because," Tomaso said, drawing himself up to his full height and taking on an official air of an authority figure, "if truffles had been transported over the border, anyone who knows of this must notify the authorities."

The guard looked at Tomaso but couldn't decide whether he was from the Italian government. Finally, he admitted that a lady had driven a truck through this spot, about two hours earlier, and she had truffles on board. The guard made up some excuse about not understanding that this was illegal – a weak excuse, but an attempt to defend his actions.

"She couldn't have had much," he lied, and carefully avoided mentioning that he had accepted a pocketful of the white diamonds in exchange for letting her go.

After his admission, the guard pleaded with Tomaso not to say anything to the authorities, and he even offered his illicit handful of truffles in payment. But Tomaso signaled no.

"It's okay. Your information is worth the truffles. Keep them," he said as he started to drive away.

Observing all this from the back of the truck, Stefano couldn't restrain his culinary instincts. As the truck began to roll down the road, with the guard still standing with his hands stretched out before him offering the truffles, Stefano called out, "Don't cook them. Just shave them onto pasta." before the truck was out of earshot.

As Lucia's car rolled past the guard, Rita shouted out the window, "They're terrific on an omelet, too!"

A few miles later, Tomaso pulled the truck to a halt and got out. Addressing the men in the back and the women in the following car, he said, "It's late. Night has overtaken us and we're not going to find Lidia this evening. I suggest we drive on to Modane, get some rooms, and begin again tomorrow."

All agreed. They were weary and not sure of success at this hour anyway. And suddenly, they all began to feel extremely hungry.

59

DINNER IN MODANE

The guard's hotel suggestions were not overly helpful, but Lucia had a few ideas. When they pulled up to the hotel she recommended and got out, Paolo shot her a glance. Lucia picked up his thought, but with a flip of her eyebrows and a knowing smile, she dismissed him.

Without bags or clean clothes, they must have been a motley crew checking into the hotel. The clerk scanned the crowd and tried to figure out how many rooms to assign. Even the new guests seemed confused at first.

"I know we get one," said Rita taking the first key offered and pulling Stefano by the hand toward the steps.

Nicki reached for the second key, but stepped forward before Francesco could read her intentions. She didn't look back as she ascended the steps, leaving Francesco behind, coming to the realization that Nicki was now lost to him.

Paolo knew that no one in the room was related to him or to Lucia, but he respected Tomaso and didn't want to insult him. The two men looked at each other for a moment until Lucia settled the matter.

Reaching for the clerk's next offered key, she took Paolo's hand and nodded to Tomaso, accepting his pardon though it hadn't yet been offered.

Tomaso shrugged his shoulders and smiled at the clerk, who offered him the last key. Tomaso turned to his wayward son, hooked his thumb in the direction of the stairs and started up. Before leaving the lobby, though, he asked the clerk for restaurant suggestions.

"It's getting late," the clerk said, consulting the clock on the wall, "but Le Tagine is very good and it's just around the corner."

Waving everyone off to their rooms, Tomaso instructed them to meet back in the lobby in ten minutes. Then, as if suddenly recalling a matter too long forgotten, Tomaso opened the front door to the hotel, whistled, and Dolce bounded in.

The clerk gulped and blurted out, "But, signore…" to which Tomaso offered only a friendly wave, thanking the man as he and Dolce bounded up the steps before the clerk could intervene.

Soon reconvened in the lobby, the group waved to the clerk and headed out for a long-awaited meal.

Le Tagine bridged the gap between simplicity and elegance, as did the choice of menu items. Rita's natural attraction to food drew her into a lengthy analysis of the dishes described, and Stefano's hunger overcame his longing for something Italian, preferably with truffles.

The wine arrived in a label-less carafe and platters of appetizers followed. Between appreciative bites and Rita's ongoing monologue about the merits of French cooking, there was much discussion about all the recent events. Alfonso's death darkened some of the conversation, as did the lingering concern about violence playing a role in their pursuit, but the excitement of the road, meeting the Zingari, and closing in on the truffles made for avid table talk.

"The Zingari are good people," Tomaso said, "but they live on the margins of society. It's no wonder they got involved with something like this."

"But they weren't involved in Alfonso's murder," Francesco said, more of a plea than a statement.

"Doubtful," remarked Lucia, whose life spent in northern Italy put her in closer contact with the Zingari and the rumors about their lifestyle. "They're decent people who prefer to live beyond the bounds of mainstream Italian life."

"More power to them," said Stefano. Rita looked at him and chuckled, unsure what to make of her husband's comments at times.

"What are we going to do tomorrow?" asked Paolo.

"I've been thinking about that and I believe we should retrace our steps a bit," said Tomaso.

"By the time we crossed the border," Francesco added, "which I'm sure Lidia also did, it was dark. If there is any evidence of her itinerary, we wouldn't have seen it tonight."

"Si," agreed his father. "I think we should drive back to the border tomorrow morning and drive along the road back here, looking for clues."

"We don't have to go all the way back," interjected Nicki. "The guard at the crossing saw Lidia driving a truck full of truffles. We only need to go that far back."

"*D'accordo*," chimed Tomaso, and they turned their attention back to the plates that were arriving at the table.

"*Un altra bottiglia di vino,*" Stefano told the waiter through a mouthful of food. "Another bottle of wine." The waiter was close enough to the Italian border to understand such simple instructions in that language, but still sniffed at the rudeness of this patron for not speaking to him in French.

Before long, the conversation turned back to truffles.

"The Périgord truffles are as expensive as the Alba truffle, right?" suggested Paolo, showing off bits of his recent education.

"Si," nodded Tomaso, but before he could finish his statement, Lucia interrupted.

"Si, but that doesn't make them better. The French market everything as better than anybody else's, wine, food, clothes, but price isn't the only measure."

"We have spent our lives in food," added Stefano, "and we've tasted both."

"And just because we're Italian doesn't mean we can't tell the difference," suggested Rita.

"But truffles are consumed all over the world," Paolo began, "why would the world pay more for the Périgord?"

"Aha!" said Tomaso, "That's where you're wrong. The French market their Périgord for more money in Europe, but in the rest of the world, the white truffle from Piedmont is *piu caro.*" It was a linguistic irony that, in Italian, the word for "expensive" was the same as the word for "dear."

Talk wound about different aspects of the truffle, including that the seasons were different for the white and the black truffles. As Tomaso pointed out, the Périgord was not even available yet – it was normally harvested in spring – and so they couldn't have had a meal with truffles that night in Le Tagine.

There was a brief silence at the table, as all realized the import of that information.

"Unless, there were white truffles around," Tomaso intoned solemnly. He called the waiter over and asked innocently if there were any items on the menu that featured fresh truffles.

"But, no, monsieur, truffles aren't here yet," the waiter gasped, clearly insulted that this foreigner would come to his restaurant and not even know that the glorious Périgord was still months away.

The waiter's rebuff didn't dissuade Stefano, though. He was the only one at the table whose nose for *tartufi* could even approach that of Dolce's. Stefano rose slowly, asked the waiter where the bathroom was, then walked a long, round-about way in that direction, in an arc that took him past the swinging door of the kitchen.

His face beamed, his eyes lit up, and he couldn't conceal his discovery from his friends at the table. He even gave an exaggerated sniff at the doorway to ferret out the evidence. Nodding his head, he signaled to the tablemates that he had certainly found the scent of *Tuber magnatum* coming from inside. Stefano returned to the table to decide what to do next.

But without pausing, Tomaso called for the waiter, saying "This meal is wonderful. We are in the restaurant business in Italy and we'd like to congratulate the chef. Is he here?"

"Oui, monsieur. Just a moment," and he left to proudly herd the chef out to this table of admiring patrons.

Admiration was not what they had in mind, though. No sooner had the chef appeared at their table then Rita began her gentle grilling.

"Chef, the food is wonderful, but my husband detected an aroma from your kitchen even more wonderful than our own food. Your dinner, no?" she said with a conspiratorial wink.

"*Oui*, a man's got to eat, of course," chef replied.

"But the smell is intoxicating," added Stefano. "It's truffles, no?"

The chef suddenly looked suspicious and glanced around the table. Even that oaf of a waiter couldn't tell what he was eating, but these people in the dining room could smell it?

"No?" Stefano repeated.

"Yes, but they are only the inferior Italian truffles," the chef said, then wanted to retract his comment in the midst of this table of Italians.

"Well, not inferior, but clearly out of season." It was clear the man would never have a career in politics.

"Where did you get *tartufi* this far from Italy?" asked Lucia. It was a bold question and without particular merit, since truffles were bartered throughout Europe and the world. But she wanted to keep the attention – and questions – directed at the chef. Raise his temperature, maybe.

The chef explained that a woman had dinner there earlier in the evening. He detected the aroma of truffles on her coat – yes, he had to emphasize to his guests, chefs <u>can</u> do that – and so he asked if she was in the truffle business. The question took her by surprise, but instead of saying no, she made up a quick story to cover herself. The chef could tell the woman's truffle enterprise wasn't for him, but he longed for the taste.

"Even the Italian kind," he said.

"What did you do?" Rita asked.

"I bought one from her. It was strange, though. She reached into her pocket and produced only a single truffle. It was so aromatic!" he exclaimed, almost losing his train of thought. "But she had only that one and yet she sold it to me. Pagan!" he spat out. "Didn't she know what she was holding?"

They got as much information as they could from chef, and realized that Lidia had been there before them, but they couldn't account for the truck. Paying the bill, Tomaso offered his thanks for the meal, and they left to return to warm, welcoming beds.

60

EVEN THE LIES ARE TRUE

The next morning, everyone rose early, even Paolo, although it took some gentle encouragement from Lucia to get him up and in the shower.

Meeting out on the sidewalk, they found a place for a quick breakfast, then returned to their vehicles to continue their quest.

"I think we should look around Modane to see if we can find Lidia," suggested Nicki, looking very much like she'd wring the woman's neck if they found her.

Before any action was taken, a French policeman approached, escorted by Captain Mussino from Alba. Inquiring looks circulated among the seven, and Dolce gave out a low growl.

"Monsieur, this is Captain Mussino from Italy," said the policeman.

"Si, we know Captain Mussino," said Tomaso, as the Italian policeman nodded and turned to the Frenchman.

"These are the people inquiring about truffles?" he asked.

"Oui, and as you can see they've stayed the night and have no luggage," he responded. "Seems suspicious, no?"

"Si, si," Mussino replied, but dismissed the thought with a wave of his hand. "I know who they are and…." surveying the group, "I know why they are here. May I speak with them alone."

"No, monsieur, this is my country, my town. I will remain."

"Okay," Mussino conceded. He then proceeded to question Tomaso and the others about their activities over the last twenty-four hours. Tomaso decided not to anger the captain by skirting the truth, so he detailed their encounter with the Zingari, their race over the border, and their encounter with the border guard. He included all the details that concern the truffle hunt, but omitted reference to Alfonso's murder, since he couldn't be sure that Mussino had shared that with the French policeman.

"So," Mussino began thoughtfully, "you haven't found the truffles, haven't found this Lidia woman, but you decided to spend the night here in Modane. Why not go home?"

"We were tired and, besides, we intended to resume the hunt today," said Francesco.

Mussino and the Frenchman conferred, then the group overheard Mussino explain that the truffles belonged to them, so there was no crime in them pursuing their own possessions. He, Mussino, had been involved in the investigation of the theft and – he added in a lowered voice – "that other matter."

Stefano was the only one close enough to hear that last whispered part, but smiled in approval of Mussino's wise maneuver. He could have concocted some fiction about his presence in France, something no doubt dark and dangerous, but without mentioning murder, and maintained the Frenchman's confidence by referring to it as "that other matter."

After a brief consultation, the two policemen turn back toward Tomaso and the others.

"Okay," began Mussino. "You can go search for your truffles; we will search for Lidia." Turning to the Frenchman for approval of the next statement, Mussino added, "Starting right here," pointing to the ground at his feet.

Such is a familiar signal among Italians and it warned Tomaso and the group to turn and be gone. Which they did without delay.

They retrieved their vehicles and made a quick exit, heading south toward the border to retrace their path from the previous evening. Modane is just off the main road, so in a few minutes they found themselves nearing the border control point.

Tomaso veered toward the shoulder of the road when he spied the post, knowing that Lidia and her truck had passed at least this far together. Lucia turned her car sharply too, to keep up with Tomaso, and the two vehicles made screeching U-turns that drew the guard's attention. They sped off, no doubt leaving suspicions in the mind of the guard whose duty it was to protect the border from illicit crossings, but they were gone before he could react.

Driving once again in the direction of Modane, Tomaso lowered his speed and everyone concentrated on the shoulders of the road and the sweeping environs on either side. It was pastoral land, mostly scrub grass, with occasional rolling hills that formed the foot of the mountains farther in the distance. The roadway and immediate shoulder had little to interest them, and it seemed like they might be wasting their time. Kilometer after kilometer rolled by through barren hills and twists and turns in the N543 highway.

The cars climbed a long hill at the base of the French Alps and arced along a curving road to the west. At the crest of the climb, they discovered a large rest stop occupied by numerous trucks and cars with foreign plates. Tomaso inquired whether anyone had to stop, and looked in his rearview mirror for acknowledgement from the ladies.

Instead of a signal he would have expected, he saw instead frantic waving from the women in Lucia's car. Rita pointed toward the left, with exaggerated hand signals, to an old canvas-covered truck that looked out of place among the eighteen-wheelers, white panel trucks, and moving vans.

Tomaso swung left and cut through the lanes to approach the truck. By the time he had brought his truck to a stop, Dolce was already bounding out of the back. Barking and signaling to the truck that Rita had indicated, Dolce drew everyone's attention, even from the unshaven drivers of the rigs parked around the lot.

Francesco and Paolo ran fastest, but Lucia easily kept up with Stefano, as the seven reached the old battered truck. Even without Dolce's help, every one of them knew that there were truffles inside the vehicle. Paolo stepped forward, pulled on the canvas back, and stared in wonderment at a dozen cloth bags tossed carelessly atop one another inside the truck. The aroma was now strong, and distinctive.

The others approached carefully, as if they were nearing sacred ground. Stefano was shaking his head in disbelief, Lucia was smiling and nearly laughing. Tomaso had his arm around Rita's shoulder, and they both were actually crying. Francesco stood back a step, hoping that this find would return him to his father's graces.

There it stood: a truck filled nearly to the brim with the world's most elusive, and most expensive, edible treasure. They stared at a trove worth untold thousands – millions? – of euros. Each entertained different dreams. Rita and Stefano were mentally scrolling through all the recipes in their portfolio, Lucia recalled the love her father had for this fungus, Tomaso simply shook his head in amazement, knowing that he had never – and never would again – witness this many *tartufi* in one place for the rest of his life.

Francesco was relieved, but couldn't dispel thoughts of Alfonso. Nicki was sure that, somehow, this was going to translate into many more truffle dishes to ferry out to the dining room of Ristorante Girasole.

Lucia tried to put it into words, to explain to Paolo how this tuber, normally seen in quantities that could barely fill your hand, was as dear to her father and her father's father as his own family. An incipient tear emerged from the corner of her eye, lingered for a second, then began a slow descent down her cheek.

"And to me, too," she added. "The *tartufo* is a culinary divinity, but it is also a firmly held tradition, a practice that bonds the Piemontese to each other, and each generation to the next. The secrets, mysteries, superstitions, even the lies told about it are all true."

As the words poured out of Lucia's mouth, the others turned to listen. She was telling the story of the *tartufi* and Alba's *trifolài* in nearly poetic terms. Lucia's monologue captivated all of them, even the long-practiced and wizened old Tomaso, who smiled back in appreciation for her stories.

Then, she stopped. She had meant for her outpouring to reach Paolo's ears only, but when she realized that everyone was standing in rapt attention, she blushed. Each of the six smiled in appreciation and hugs swept the crowd.

"Where is Lidia?" Rita asked, looking around for some sign of a guardian for this treasure.

But when they realized that their activities had gathered a crowd of truck drivers, they reverted to the present and quickly summed up a plan of action.

"Let's drive the truck back to Alba," Tomaso said, but then added, "we may have to bribe the guard again."

"Why would Lidia just leave the truffles out here?" Rita continued, as she and the others looked around scanning the parking lot for her.

"I don't know," replied Tomaso, "but it won't help us to just sit here and wait for her to return."

Turning to Francesco, Tomaso then asked, "Do you still remember how to jump a truck engine?"

Nicki scowled, but Tomaso just laughed.

"We have a truck at the vegetable garden that has no keys," he laughed. "They were lost long ago, so we just leave the two wires dangling below the dashboard and just start the engine by connecting them."

Francesco climbed under the dashboard of the truck, reached up and pulled a handful of wires down. Separating the ones that didn't matter, he found the two that would do the trick. With a spark and a quick twist of the wrist, the motor roared to life.

He then climed into the driver's seat and Paolo joined him. Tomaso and Stefano got in Tomaso's truck, and the women joined up in Lucia's car. Then they left in a caravan, heading back along highway N543 toward the Italian border.

61

HEADING HOME

As they approached the border, they slowed to a stop. There were two vehicles stopped up ahead and Francesco, in the lead vehicle, strained to see who was standing beside them. The blue uniforms of two individuals were clear enough, although one wore a braid over the shoulder and the other didn't.

"That's Mussino and his French companion," said Francesco, recognizing the cut and color of the municipal police uniform from Alba.

"What are they doing?" asked Paolo.

"Can't tell."

By that time, Tomaso had left his truck and walked past Francesco in his, and strode up to the police car ahead. Francesco and Paolo watched Tomaso converse with the police, then he looked back at them and drew a finger across his throat. Resuming his conversation with the police, Tomaso waved his hands, raised his shoulders, and shook his head back and forth. Finally, he nodded... once, twice, then he turned to go back to his truck.

Passing Francesco who still sat with his hands on the wheel, he explained.

"Mussino and the Frenchman caught up to Lidia in Modane this morning, what was left of her. She had a zappino buried halfway into her chest."

Rita, Nicki, and Lucia had left their car to hear what Tomaso had to say, and Stefano was close behind.

"They also had a watch out for her car. They arrested a guy, Ruger Klein, driving it. Didn't think much at first but it was a police K-9 unit that saw him. As the police officer was questioning this Klein guy, the dog in the back was going berserk," Tomaso continued.

"Finally," Tomaso said, "they let the dog out and he runs straight for the trunk of the guy's car and barks and jumps around.

"What was it?" asked Rita.

"Cocaine. Lots of it. Kilos and kilos of the stuff. It filled the trunk. Must've been millions of euros worth.

"So the truffles?" asked Francesco, almost sheepishly.

"When I explained to Mussino that we had found the truffles, abandoned, he was confused. But then we realized that the truffles were only being used as a cover for smuggling the cocaine.

"The aroma!" said Stefano.

"Si," Lucia added, "the aroma would have covered up the smell of cocaine. It would make it easier to get past the guard dogs at the border."

"Just like the border guard told us last night," Nicki recalled. "That's why he was bought off with what he thought were just innocent truffles, not cocaine."

"So this whole thing, Alfonso's computer program, Lucia's plot to steal the crop, Alfonso's death, and now Lidia's, was all so that Lidia and Ruger could smuggle drugs across the border and," adding with a sudden look of panic, "then ditch a hoard of truffles at a truck stop!?"

"Sounds like it. All along they planned to abandon the truffles and drive off with the cocaine," added Nicki. "But I guess Ruger wasn't very good at sharing."

"Si. They probably met with the getaway car in the parking lot of the rest stop, transferred the cocaine from the truck at night, then drove off with their treasure, leaving the truffles behind."

"How are the Zingari involved?" asked Paolo.

"I think Lidia wanted to cover her tracks," Tomaso said, "so she didn't want to be seen driving the truck away. Besides she needed another driver and maybe she didn't trust Ruger." All heads nodded at that, without surprise.

"She lured the Zingari into her plot," Tomaso continued, "without telling them everything, and got them to drive the truck away. This is exactly what the witness told Mussino, about the truck parked outside the warehouse. By hiring the Zingari, she avoided detection, then met with them outside of Bordanecchia, and drove off with the truffles."

With dead bodies scattered throughout Italy, they would never find out that the cocaine had been smuggled first from North Africa into Genoa, then driven north to Alba.

"Ruger must have caught up with her in Modane, killed her for the truffles and cocaine, and would have gotten away except for that K-9 unit," Paolo said. "Lucky that they had a bulletin out for her, lucky that the stop was by a K-9 unit, and lucky that they stopped long enough to search his car."

"Yeah, lucky day," said Stefano, "not so lucky for Ruger."

"A zappino, though?" remarked Rita, almost smiling in wry satisfaction at the irony.

"Si," said Tomaso, "the police said Ruger bragged that he knew a lot about truffles. That he had been hunting them for weeks and he deserved to keep those he found. I'm sure his fingerprints will end up on the zappino they found in Lidia's chest."

"What about us?" Lucia asked.

"The French policeman said we can cross back over into Italy. Of course, I had to promise him a few truffles first." And everyone laughed when Tomaso relayed how the Frenchman couldn't be all bad. "He admitted that he preferred Alba's white truffle to the Périgord anyway," and everyone laughed.

They rejoined their vehicles and proceeded to the checkpoint. Slowing to a stop, Francesco reminded the guard what he had heard about being able to pass through. The guard waved him on by, but stopped Tomaso driving his truck.

Francesco paused with a worried look on his face as his father was detained, then smiled broadly when he saw Tomaso's hand emerge through the open window with his palm open and up-raised. Francesco saw the guard reach toward Tomaso's hand, close his fingers around something, and withdraw.

"Ah, yes, the truffle tax," he murmured, and Paolo laughed too.

62

RETURN TO ALBA

The passengers of the three vehicles were more relaxed and more talkative on the drive back to Alba. Finding the truffles had been an unexpected victory, even discovering that Lidia had been dispatched with a truffle-digging stick didn't dampen their spirits.

But the conversation in each truck and car followed the same course.

"What will we do with the truffles?" Paolo asked Francesco.

"I don't know. There's a fortune piled up behind us," jabbing his thumb over his shoulder at the truck bed, "but we can't claim it for ourselves."

They sat in silence for a moment, each apparently trying to figure out the solution.

"We can't put them back in the ground," Paolo said, pointlessly.

Francesco looked at him with a look of disbelief.

Another moment of silence while Francesco looked in the side view mirror at the vehicles following them.

"We could distribute the *tartufi* among the hunters," Paolo offered, although he couldn't exactly phrase how to do that. "But they don't all get the same amount."

"No," Francesco said, "each *trifolào* has his own fields and harvests different amounts. The traditions and *conoscenza* of the region," he said, referring to the awareness that Albese have of the hunters, "give us an idea of how much each hunter usually brings in. We could create some sort of formula and distribute the truffles that way."

"But that would result in fights and arguments, no?" said Paolo.

Francesco retreated to silence again and remained that way for most of the return trip. Paolo looked out the front of the truck, as if he was studying the road ahead, but his thoughts were clearly on the cache of truffles that sat behind him. He inhaled deeply at one point, luxuriating in the heady scent of truffles, and his thoughts turned to his life and what had happened to him in the recent weeks.

His mother had sent him to visit Rita and work in her restaurant. Catrina no doubt imagined the sojourn would be a learning experience, but she couldn't have anticipated the lessons her son would actually collect.

Paolo chuckled to himself as he recalled the donkeys in the Palio degli Asini, how they would buck and dawdle while their riders tried to urge them on. And he recalled the meals, the many delicious dishes and new flavors that had passed his palate. The stupendous wines, the scent of truffles, and the eye-opening aroma of fresh espresso on a misty morning in Alba.

As the truck rumbled over rutted roads outside Alba and Paolo saw the skyline of the ancient city come into view, he thought more about the food of the region. His mouth watered as he rekindled memories of the pappardelle, the buttery sauces more common in this northern region than in his hometown in Tuscany, the succulent meats, and the herb-infused vegetables that accompanied every meal.

His lips grew moist and his mouth watered at the thought of the fabulous Barolo and Barbaresco wines he had sampled here. He would never forget the white wines like Arneis and Cortese, but it was the regal reds of Piedmont that most captured his imagination.

"True," he mumbled, then saw Francesco look over at him quizzically. True that his mother didn't realize what an adventure she had sent him out on.

Debates continued in the other vehicles as well. Rita, Lucia, and Nicki were hotly arguing who the truffles belonged to.

"They belong to the *trifolài*," said Lucia, daughter of one.

"Of course they do," agreed Rita, but she pointed out that most of the *trifolài* wouldn't talk to the authorities about their crop, so how would the bounty be returned to them.

"I think we should bring the *tartufi* to the market," said Nicki. "Once they were sold, we would distribute the money. That way we could disconnect the value that was being shared with the truffle hunters from the crop itself. The *fisco* would be fooled and couldn't accuse the hunters of avoiding their taxes."

"But the *fisco* would want to know where the money came from," argued Rita, "besides don't you think the *fisco* would wonder where a truckload of truffles came from?"

And so it went the rest of the way into town.

But wise Tomaso wasn't at all confused about the way to handle the sudden treasure trove of the world's most expensive ingredient.

63

THE ONLY SOLUTION

Just before dinner, the three vehicles pulled into Alba. First, they veered to the west side of town where Tomaso kept his warehouse to store the farm produce. He parked the truffle-laden truck in the warehouse, locked the doors, then climbed into the back of his own truck which Francesco still piloted. Stefano joined him in the back, and the four men waved for the women to follow in Lucia's car.

Francesco weaved through evening traffic to Vincafé. They climbed from the vehicles and entered the restaurant. Tomaso went up to the owner and said, "See, I told you we'd return." And the seven were seated at the same table they had abandoned at lunch the day before, a meal that now seemed like it had happened weeks ago.

Once chilled bottles of Prosecco and Arneis were delivered, the conversation veered toward how to solve their problem with the truffles. Ideas were flung from every perspective, whether honoring the labors of the *trifolài*, avoiding detection by the *fisco*, sharing the wealth with the restaurants, managing to preserve the dignity and tradition of Alba's truffles, even punishing those who caused this disaster.

"The criminals have already been brought to justice.... of a sort," explained Stefano, to a chorus of nodding heads.

At one point, Francesco realized that in the midst of this cacophony, his father was the only one who hadn't expressed an opinion. So he turned to him and asked what he would do.

Tomaso surveyed the table, poured another glass of wine, then signaled to the waiter to bring a bottle of Ceretto Barolo Brunate, one of the Piedmont's most exquisite wines. Stefano smiled, Lucia nodded in recognition, and Rita licked her lips. Paolo, sitting between Nicki and Lucia had already learned much about the local wines, and he knew that this Ceretto was a classic. He let out a soft yet audible gasp at Tomaso's order which brought smiles from the others and gentle elbow to the ribs from Lucia.

"Papa, what would you do?" asked Francesco.

Tomaso spoke without hesitation, and with conviction.

"Two thirds of the truffle hoard will be distributed among the regular customers of mine and the other *trifolài* in Alba. I know everyone and, despite the secrecy, we know about how much each hunter usually brings in. The *trifolài* will be told that, to receive their share, these truffles must be given to their customers like restaurants and regular buyers for free," and he paused to let this sink in.

"Free," he repeated, lest anyone had missed his point.

Anticipating the questions and objections, Tomaso plowed ahead. "We have all taken a loss, but we have also sold truffles this year for a higher price than usual. By sharing these with our customers, we will regain their trust and only suffer a modest loss of annual revenue. We will count on the traditions of the black market to prevent anyone from questioning the sudden largesse or contact the authorities. And all will benefit from the windfall."

He paused again, and watched as the meaning sank in. Heads nodded, and faces around the table seemed to brighten up at this straightforward solution.

"The other third of the truffles will be given to Rita and Stefano to serve at their restaurant in Genoa."

Francesco objected, though only lightly so as not to alienate his friends at the table.

"Papa, I'm sure they would be delighted to have these truffles, but one-third?"

"They put pressure on us all to keep this investigation alive, questioning *trifolài*, their customers, even the police to make sure we didn't give up on this. And without Paolo's help," here Tomaso nodded at the young man he had come to love and respect, "and Nicki's persistence while Rita and Stefano were forced to return to Genoa, we might never have uncovered this evil deed."

Tomaso spoke these last two words while staring directly into his son's eyes, a son who then cast his guilty gaze downward. Everyone at the table knew that Francesco was swept innocently into this criminal act, but they also knew his actions made the theft possible. With some reservations and a wealth of tolerance, they were able to forgive Francesco's actions, but he would live with the guilt for a long time.

Just then, when Francesco's face still burned from shame and embarrassment, his father chose to deliver his most solemn declaration.

"And Francesco," his voice nearly boomed. "What of you? Will you continue to lead an easy life of pleasure, or will you settle down and help me with the farm?"

Francesco looked at his father and realized that this was not a question as much as a command. He had enjoyed his youth, and plied his good looks, but he was also growing into a man. *My father is right*, he thought to himself, while he also realized that family was the bond that held Italian society together.

Paolo searched Francesco's face to somehow glean the emotions that swirled through his friend's heart and mind at that moment. He knew that Francesco would obey his father; that's what Italian men did. At that thought, Paolo nearly began crying, thinking of his own father in the vineyard in Sinalunga.

"Si, papa," began Francesco slowly. "It is time that the family farm is worked by the entire family."

Tomaso offered the proud smile only a father can possess.

"Si," Francesco repeated, with a surreptitious look in Nicki's direction. She was drinking from her wine glass, uninterested in the conversation, and obviously uninterested in Francesco. He knew he had lost her.

64

A CLASH, AND AN AGREEMENT

Tomaso called a meeting of the *trifolài* at the Castello Grinzane Cavour, the fraternity quarters of the Ordine dei Cavalieri del Tartufo e Vino. He began by reporting on the events of the last few days, and made sure that the gathering of hunters was fully apprised of the successful work of the group from the Ristorante Girasole.

When he announced that the truffles had been recovered, there was a roar so loud it threatened to bring down the ancient walls of the building where they met. Then, in careful detail, Tomaso laid out his plans for redistributing them. He said some were given to Rita and Stefano, without detailing how much, then said the remainder would be shared with the regular customers of those gathered, for free.

Looks of disbelief and cries of anguish from the crowd were accompanied by worried glances and accusations of what some quickly named a "second" theft. Tomaso raised his arms and tried to quiet the mass before him, repeating many of his earlier remarks about the secrecy of their work, the greed of the *fisco*, the risks of discovery, and the need to re-establish the reputation of the Tartufo d'Alba. He also reminded them of the importance of regaining the market for the next year, and regaining the trust of the buyers.

New looks appeared on faces throughout the crowd. There were still some doubtful glances and some shaking heads, but the consensus was beginning to shift.

"How many truffles were found?"

Tomaso described the quantity in kilos, summing up the two-thirds that remained only. The hunters in the room huffed and sighed, but no one offered a different plan. This all-against-one debate continued for nearly two hours, but in the end the gathering agreed to Tomaso's plan.

65

BACK TO GENOA

Rita, Stefano, and Nicki left for the train station the next morning. Francesco was nowhere to be seen, which suited Nicki just fine. Paolo commandeered the truck with the truffles back to Genoa.

Just before pulling away from the curb, Lucia drove up in her car.

"So, you're returning to Genoa," she said.

"Si, but from there to Sinalunga. That's where I belong," he responded.

Lucia gave him a long look, and a longer kiss.

"Just as I belong here in Alba," was all she could say. With that, she turned back to her car, started the engine, and waved lightly at Paolo as she drove away.

On the train ride back home, Rita couldn't take her mind off of truffle recipes. Stefano had bigger ideas, which he wouldn't reveal to Rita until later.

When the train pulled into the station on Piazza Acquaverde, Paolo was waiting for them.

"I've already delivered the truffles to the restaurant," he said, whispering his news as if a stranger might be spying on them.

The four of them squeezed into a single taxi for the ride back to the Ristorante Girasole. On the way home, Rita talked about all that had to be done, and the preparations that she would have to make to manage all the truffles that now awaited them at the restaurant. She noticed, but didn't pay much attention to, the smug look on Stefano's face.

As they neared the Ristorante Girasole, Rita noticed a long, rolled up cloth above the doors that stretched from one end to the other. She craned her neck to see it better as the taxi pulled up to the curb, then alighted on the sidewalk.

Rita had her hands on her hips when the other taxi pulled up, and she looked sternly now at Stefano's grinning face. Nicki and Paolo were standing beside them before Stefano made any move. Then he walked up to the front of the restaurant, gripped a thin rope that dangled from one end of the furled cloth, and gave it a sharp tug.

As the cloth unrolled, Rita gave out a little shriek of pleasure, clapping her hands over her mouth as she did so. Below the ornate lettering of the Ristorante Girasole's original sign, the new cloth banner declared it to be "La Casa del Tartufo."

Stefano's grin spread across his face as he saw the effect this had on his wife. She wrapped her arms around his neck and planted a moist kiss on his cheek.

They spent the next day re-organizing the menu and cleaning up the place for re-opening that night. It was a busy evening, especially as pedestrians and regulars took note of the new name on the banner. Rita and Stefano couldn't have wished for a more propitious night than this first one as "La Casa del Tartufo."

Later, exhausted from serving more plates than ever before, the five gathered at their own table in the kitchen after closing. Rita and Stefano chattered non-stop about the truffle hunt and Nicki offered her own version of the tales. Rita ticked off new ideas for recipes on her fingers, and her detailed description of the flavors made Paolo's mouth water.

Stefano gathered up some of the plates and offered to begin washing them. He disappeared into the kitchen and they could hear the sound of water filling the stainless steel sinks behind the swinging doors. Rita sooned joined him, leaving Paolo and Nicki alone.

"I belong here too," said Nicki, as she stood to join her adopted family in the kitchen.

Paolo sat alone for a few more minutes, enjoying the last of the great wine in his glass, and comparing it to the equally fabulous wines from his own region. His mind wandered helter skelter from Piedmont to Tuscany, from Barolo to Chianti, and from this close-knit family to his own in Sinalunga.

Then he stacked his own plates and headed for the kitchen.

66

HEADING HOME TO SINALUNGA

Paolo was packing his bags the next morning, gathering his belongings on the bed in Rita's house where he had stayed the last two weeks. He opened the door to find Nicki and his aunt just as she was raising her hand to knock.

With a shared laugh, she lowered her hand and smiled at Paolo.

"So, you're leaving," said Nicki.

"Si, but I will return many times."

Hugs with each of the women were followed by instructions from Rita.

"You sound like mama," Paolo kidded her and, with that, the normally strong and purposeful Rita began to cry. She didn't have children and Paolo was too old to fill that role anyway, but he had been in her charge and she had come to treat him as the closest of family.

Stefano drove him to the train station and hugged him for a long moment before departure. Paolo stepped back, thanked Stefano for all he had learned, and promised that he would not soon forget the wines and food of the Piemontese.

"How could you forget!" was the proud response.

At the other end of the train ride, Paolo disembarked onto the platform. He stood there alone, for he decided not to alert his parents of his return trip. He gazed at the familiar surroundings at the Arezzo station, then picked up his bag and caught a bus that would take him to Sinalunga.

The bus ride dropped him off two miles from the farm, but Paolo was still reluctant to break the quiet of his return, so he hitched a ride from an old man driving a farm truck in the direction of the dell'Uco farm.

Jumping down from the truck at the end of his own driveway, Paolo saluted the driver and turned to walk the last quarter mile toward the vineyard. There was a slight hill as he approached, which hid the view of the vineyard at first, but as he mounted it and surpassed the peak, the brownish-gray of the vines of autumn spanned out before him.

Paolo stood for a moment at the crest, looking from left to right, taking in the breadth of the vineyard his father tended. There were thousands of vines producing high quality grapes, fruit that went into someone else's fermenter, to bottle the wine and slake the thirst of those who understood and appreciated the best wines of Tuscany.

After heaving a sigh of relief at being home, Paolo strode down the path toward the vines. It was about mid-afternoon, too early for his father to have retired yet, so he expected to find Dito wandering through the rows. There might be less to do after the harvest, but Paolo knew his father would be there among his "children."

Suddenly, Paolo stopped. He saw his father bent down between two vines, inspecting the late autumn growth and fingering the shoots that had not yet been pruned.

As if he sensed someone staring at him, Dito rose and turned in Paolo's direction. His face lit up with the recognition of his visitor and, although running to his son would have been unbecoming, Dito opened his arms wide to welcome Paolo home.

They hugged and exchanged familial words, and Paolo gave only a sketch of the events, a sketch that he was anxious to fill in while feasting on one of his mother's dinners that night.

"I want to come home, papa," Paolo said, and his father beamed with pride and appreciation.

"But I want to make wine, not just grow the grapes."

It was this last pronouncement that hit Dito suddenly. He had made a good living growing and selling his grapes. For a brief moment he wondered whether his son's statement was a criticism of the life Dito had chosen, but he was convinced by the loving look in his son's eyes that it wasn't that at all.

Life goes on and the world changes. Dito recalled when he told his own father that he didn't want to grow crops, as his father had done. He wanted to grow grapes.

"How can you make a living with just grapes," Dito remembered his father saying.

With a smile of understanding, Dito decided that his own son's declaration was no different than his own.

Besides, at least it meant that Paolo would stay in Sinalunga.

CPSIA information can be obtained
at www.ICGtesting.com
Printed in the USA
LVOW01s2123011115
460683LV00009B/53/P